Just When . . .

Just When . . .

G. L. Johnson

authorHOUSE®

AuthorHouse™
1663 Liberty Drive
Bloomington, IN 47403
www.authorhouse.com
Phone: 1-800-839-8640

Published by AuthorHouse   07/31/2012

ISBN: 978-1-4772-4503-3 (sc)
ISBN: 978-1-4772-4504-0 (e)

Library of Congress Control Number: 2012912788

Editor- Kia Smith
Kia@IamKiaSpeaks.com

Cover Designer- Britney Bryant
Britneybryant@ymail.com

Author- G. L. Johnson
Garyljohnson30@yahoo.com

ACKNOWLEDGMENTS

J am a true believer that everything happens for a reason. It's been a long time coming but I feel that now I am doing exactly what God planned for me to do. This book coming to fruition has truly taught me that you have to go out and make life happen it won't just happen for you! I have learned to be the most authentic me as I can be, and to cherish every person that comes into my life, because God has placed them there for a reason.

I would like to dedicated this book to the memory of my little brother Gardale "Lamar" Johnson. I can still remember you calling my name "Gayeee" when you couldn't pronounce "R's. The admiration and trust that you had in me can never be duplicated and I am glad I was able to be your big brother! I miss you today just as much as I missed you yesterday, and I can only pray that one day I will see you again!

There are so many people who I need to thank, and I'm sure I'll miss some of you. Just know that I am truly grateful for everyone who has played a role in my life. Every moment of my life good and bad has led me to this tremendous event and I am thankful.

Let me first start by thanking the people who gave me the inspiration for my book. This book would not have come to pass without my guys! Chris, Terrell, Robert, Raydale, Marcquez and Donella. All of you guys mean the world to me and I thank you for being great friends.

My best friend Tolandra Coleman. No matter how many states we may have between us or how many weeks we may go without calling, we always come back to the same comfortable place, of friendship. I know that whatever I do in life you will support me without prejudice.

I am a product of my family and I thank all of you, it really took a village to raise me and I am proud to call myself a Johnson! All of my aunts, uncles, cousins, brothers, sisters, and grandparents thank you. My cousin Kesha Johnson, we aren't as close as we used to be, but I cherish every memory we have. As a child you saved me from the insane world I was living in and you introduced to me the joys reading could bring you. I owe a big part of my literary career to you, and I want you to know that I love and cherish you dearly. My Grandmother "Frances" you gave me a strong foundation to grow from and I walk by faith because of what you taught me! Thank you for loving me when I thought no one else did! My father, through everything that you have been through in life you have always put your kids first, I am so grateful because most fathers walk out when it gets hard, and you didn't! My mother, your road has been difficult but your love is unwavering, even though I don't always show it, I love you to no end.

All of the people that pushed me to get the job done, I thank you for motivating and keeping me on task! Scottye White you pushed me to go for my dreams and I will always be grateful! Joining the KSU Housing team has opened up so many doors that I never thought possible and I appreciate each and every one of you guys! My book designer, Britney Bryant your work was impeccable! My editor, Kia Smith God placed you in my life at the right time and I look forward to a wonderful working future, (the best darn editor there ever was).

My biggest supporter, Joeanna Johnson affectionately named "Black Gold" by my mother. You are certainly my best cousin, but you have also played the role of big sister and best friend. You are truly my confidant, without you there would be no Just When . . . You have been there for every major event in my life from high school graduation, all the way to this point and I thank God everyday for having you in my life! And of course if I'm thanking Joe, I got to thank her crew! Because you guys all treat me like family and I love you guys for supporting me, Tosha, Dyonne, and Paris. You guys are all true examples of what friendship is all about, just be prepared for me to write a book about you guys!

There are so many emotions that are rolling around inside of me. I'm scared, hopeful, delighted but most of all I am grateful to God for allowing me to do something that I truly enjoy! I hope you enjoy reading Just When . . . Just as much as I enjoyed writing it!

Be Blessed!
Gary L. Johnson

PROLOGUE

"Sit up, Tristan. Sit up and take a drink." I was very groggy and out of it, but that was the first thing I heard when I woke up, the sound of my mother's voice. As I focused my eyes, I could make out her silhouette. Tiny and petite with the short bob cut she had been wearing for twenty years now. She had a cup of water in her hands and was trying to get me to drink. Although my mouth was as dry as cotton balls, I was in no mood to drink. I wanted answers. Where was I? How did I get here? What was my mother doing here? Don't get me wrong. I loved my mother's visits, but I lived in Atlanta, and she lived in Nebraska. That's not exactly around the corner.

As I looked around the room to check my surroundings, I noticed lots of flowers lined up against a pale green wall. I looked down and noticed an IV coming out of my left hand. I realized I was in the hospital. *Oh my God! What the hell was going on?* I rose up quickly, maybe a little too quickly because I became lightheaded and fell back against the crisp white pillow. My mother rushed to me. "Tristan, take your time, honey. It's okay, baby. Take your time." As my mother caressed my head, I could smell the sweet scent of her perfume. That smell of a fresh summer day and wild flowers had put me at ease ever since I was a baby. She pulled me into her arms and began to rock me back and forth; as she rocked me to dreamland, I felt a tear drop on my forehead. As my mother held me in her arms and cried, everything came rushing back to me like a tidal wave of memories. I remembered how I ended up in the hospital, all the bad things that had led up to now.

CHAPTER 1

Tristan

My name is Tristan Smith. I was born in a little town called Omaha, Nebraska. My mother, Rita Smith, a hard-working single mom, raised me and my little brother, Corey. We weren't exactly poor, but we were far from rich. My mother worked as an assistant school teacher for the neighborhood elementary school. My father left us long before I could remember. In the earlier years of my life, my father would come by and visit ever so often; however, as I got older, the visits became few and far between. Eventually, the visits stopped all together. The last I heard he was living in California with a whole new family. I was okay with that because my mother did an excellent job of raising her two sons.

Corey is two and a half years younger than me, and he chose to take a different path in life. He recently turned twenty-one and has two kids: one four months old and the other just turning four years old. The kids are by two different women. Although he did graduate high school, he opted not to go to college. Right after graduation he went to work for a printing company in our hometown and moved in with his girlfriend. Corey's work ethic is great. I attribute that to our mother. But his money management is horrible. Constantly borrowing money from either our mother or me to support one of his many habits, like drinking and gambling, Corey seemed to always stay in trouble. But I love him just the same. Growing up black and strapped for money, you learn that family is the most important thing in life. So my brother and I grew up close.

I noticed early on there was a difference between Corey and me. I was the bookworm, and he was the jock. I wasn't interested in any of the girls in my neighborhood, and my brother couldn't get enough of them. I think my mother noticed early on as well because she always made it a point to put me at ease. She would say, "Baby, you can be anything you want as long as you are happy." So at eighteen when I announced that I was gay, it was no surprise. My mother just gave me that look that said "everything is all right." My brother, who was fifteen at the time and already experimenting with girls, handled it a little differently.

"Bro, you mean you don't like the ladies? Why not?" he asked. I tried my best to explain, but he still looked confused. Later he expressed that he still loved me, and he would beat up anyone who had something to say. I pushed him down and said, "Boy, with yo scrawny self, you can't bust a grape." He proceeded to show me his newly formed muscles which the girls were beginning to notice. That was life until eighteen, not much drama and decent by most standards.

I met my first lover as a freshman in college. He was five years older than me and worked in the cafeteria of the university. He was tall, dark, and handsome with a smile that would knock you out. He was the one who forced me to come out of the closet; he forced me into a lot of things during the course of a few years. All through college we dated. His name was Jonathan, and, not to sound cliché or anything but, he loved to run game. He put me through some of the worst times of my life. He cheated on me and borrowed money that he never repaid. I even allowed him to move into the studio apartment I had my senior year in college. What a mistake that was! Shortly after he moved in, we broke up.

Over the course of my college years, I became good friends with a guy named Rashawn Meeks. Rashawn was a suave, know-it-all, take no mess kind of man. He would cuss you out at the drop of a dime and be your best friend two seconds later. We met one day as I sat in the library trying to study. He came up to me with the biggest grin and sat down in front of me. "Thank God I finally found a sista gurl here at the ole white man's campus!" I looked at him with a confused glare. "Gurl," he said, "don't be giving me no sideways look. My name is Rashawn. What's yo name?" We have been good friends ever since. In fact, Rashawn was the one who talked me into leaving Jonathan when I was visiting him in Atlanta. Rashawn had recently moved there, and I was on spring break.

"Child, you need to leave Jonathan's ass alone. You know I got the tea. He's been sleepin' with that stank hoe Marcus." Rashawn was referring to Marcus Miller, the town slut. It was crazy how even though Rashawn no longer lived in Nebraska he always knew the dirt. "After you graduate this spring, you need to pack up and move here. You can be my roommate. I got all this space."

He stood up and stretched his arms out as if displaying how much room he had available at his home. Rashawn did have a nice place. He lived off Tenth Street right across from Piedmont Park. It was a sprawling two bedroom townhome. Rashawn was an interior decorator. He was a couple of years older than me and was doing quite well. As I looked around, I became excited about the thought of being single and living in Atlanta. Of course I would hate to leave my mother and brother, but it was time to spread my wings. That night I got on the internet and started looking for jobs.

Later that spring, I graduated from the University of Nebraska with honors. With my new degree in public relations in hand, my mother shipped me off to Atlanta. My Dodge Neon was packed to the brim with my belongings. I had $4,000 in my pocket and several job interviews lined up. I arrived in Atlanta on a hot summer day in June. I was twenty-three years old and excited about the new life that lay ahead of me.

I left Jonathan with little fuss; he was in fact screwing Marcus. So I simply packed up all his things one day while he was at work and took them to Marcus's doorstep. I figured if Marcus wanted him, he could have all of him. Jonathan tried to call, apologize, and beg me not to leave, but my mind was made up. I drove down the interstate leaving my past behind, ready to make a new life in Atlanta.

My first day in Atlanta was mixed with dozens of emotions. I pulled up to Rashawn's townhome to a frenzy of commotion. There were balloons on the outside patio and a huge "Welcome to Atlanta" sign hanging over the door. The sound of Ludacris's "Welcome to Atlanta" blared through the windows of the townhouse. As I got out the car, Rashawn came running down the front stairs.

"What's all this?" I asked as we embraced.

"Child, you know I had to welcome you in style. I threw you a party and invited some of my good Judies."

Judy was gay lingo for friend; prior to moving to Atlanta, Rashawn had given me a crash course on the terminology of Atlanta. Rashawn had only been in Atlanta for a year, but he had managed to become friends with half of the city. It's no wonder why; he was hilarious, attractive, and stylish. Today, he wore his shoulder length dreads tied back in a bun. His slender figure looked well in his stylish 7 for All Mankind Jeans and button down Prada shirt. His skin was a caramel brown, and he had sparkling grey eyes. He grabbed my hand and pulled me up the front steps leaving my luggage in the car.

We entered the front door, and I was greeted by several of Rashawn's good Judies. "Let me introduce you to the Sunday Brunch Club," Rashawn said. The Sunday Brunch Club, I would later learn, was a group of friends that got together every Sunday for brunch after church. Rashawn was the self-proclaimed leader of the group. Then there was Tyler, the chubby queen of the bunch. He worked as a customer service agent for AT&T. Also in the group was Eric, who tried to be straight, but you knew he was gay the minute he talked. He and Tyler were best friends. Eric was a hospital employee at Grady Memorial, and I think he was hitting on me when we met. Finally, there was Kim. Kim was a beautiful, heterosexual, young woman from Decatur. Her hair fell just at her shoulders and swayed with every move of her neck. Her skin was a deep chocolate that shimmered under the soft light. She was thick in all the right places, her hips showing that she had bore a child. I was immediately drawn to her.

"Hi, Tristan, I'm so glad to meet you," she said in a sweet angelic voice. Her scent floated up my nostrils and had me in a trance. She smelled of freshly picked flowers.

"Child, quit staring at the girl," Rashawn said as he led me to the living room.

The house was decorated immaculately. The living room had a huge bay window, the walls were painted a soft burgundy, and there was a sectional with oversized pillows in the center of the room. A plasma television hung from one wall, and the stereo playing Ludacris was just underneath it. In the back of the townhouse, there was the dining area with a huge oak dining table that led to the galley style kitchen. Upstairs there were two bedrooms. The master bedroom, which of course was Rashawn's, had a huge canopy bed and lots of drapes hanging on the windows. Across the hall was the spare bedroom where I was making my home. We both had our own bathrooms in our rooms, and there was a half bath downstairs on the main floor. After I met everyone, we gathered on the sectional and sipped wine as I learned all about the Sunday Brunch Club.

~~~

The next morning I awoke to the smell of eggs and bacon cooking. I looked at my clock. It was 7:15 a.m.; my first interview was scheduled for 9:30 a.m. I walked downstairs where I found Rashawn standing at the kitchen stove whipping up breakfast. He was already dressed in pinstriped slacks and a tailored shirt.

"Wow, what time did you get up?" I asked sleep still in my voice.

"I have an eight o'clock client to meet. You can't sleep on money, honey," he said as he set a full plate in front of me. With that he was off. He grabbed his jacket and wished me luck as he raced out the front door, leaving me behind to get ready for the day.

I gobbled down the enormous breakfast before returning upstairs to get ready. I picked out my best suit, a blue three piece with a yellow tie. I grabbed a couple of résumés and my keys and headed out. I had three interviews scheduled for that day. I walked out the door with all the optimism in the world. I came back that evening with a little less optimism and a huge dose of reality.

All three interviews were a bust. The first one was at the Coca-Cola Company as an account manager intern. The pay was only $13 an hour and at least ten other people were there to interview for only one slot. The second interview was for a sales position which advertised $60,000 a year, but in reality they wanted you to stand on the street and sell children's toys for commission. The last one wasn't even worth sticking around for. It was located in a seedy building in downtown Atlanta. The receptionist was smoking a cigarette and dressed like she was going to be in one of TI's rap videos. When she looked me up and down and rolled her eyes, I just turned around and walked out the door.

I knew it would be hard to find a job, but I never thought it would be like this. I guess I had to remember that I was now a little fish swimming in a very huge, overpopulated pond called Atlanta. Defeated for the day, I decided to call it quits. It was about 4:30 p.m., so I headed home before the traffic got too bad.

As I pulled up to the townhouse, I noticed a black Acura parked where Rashawn's car had been parked the day before. I knew it wasn't Rashawn's because he drove a Maxima. Plus, he wasn't due home until around six. As I got out of my car, the Acura's car door opened; the sounds of Tamia's album came flooding out. The windows were tinted, so I couldn't see who was in the car. As the legs of the person in the car planted themselves on the cement, I immediately knew who it was.

Kim arose from her vehicle looking fresh to death. Wearing a full length denim skirt with high heels and a tank top blouse that barely covered her ample breast, she looked more like a supermodel with her oversized sunglasses. "Hey, Trey," she said. She barely knew me, but already had a nickname for me. That was just the personality she had. I waved and walked toward her.

"Hey, Kim! How are you doing?"

"I'm good," she said with the brightest smile in the world. We embraced, and she followed me up the front steps. "Where's Rashawn? I came by because I was in the area I thought I'd pay you guys a visit before I picked my son up from my mother's." As we walked in the door, I took my jacket off and kicked off my shoes.

"He's not home from work yet. He probably had a late client." I began to loosen my necktie. "Would you like something to drink?"

"No, thank you, baby," she said in that sweet voice. "My, don't you look nice today," she said admiring my blue suit.

"Well, you know I try," I said blushing. "I had a couple of interviews today." I plopped down on the sofa and propped my feet on the coffee table. Kim sat next to me. Boy, if I was straight she would be just my type I thought to myself.

"Well, how did they go?" she asked me.

I sighed as if I was truly worn out; "Not so well. In fact, I think I need a drink." I jumped up and went to the minibar to mix a drink. As I sipped my early evening cocktail, Kim and I chatted and got to know each other better. She was twenty-six and the mother of a beautiful five-year-old boy named Jamal. Of course she showed me pictures. She currently lived in her hometown of Decatur and had big dreams but was sidetracked by Kevin, her no good baby daddy.

Kevin was her high school sweetheart, and they still dated off and on. He was a self-proclaimed drug dealer that went back and forth to jail. Kim had just about enough of Kevin's mess. In fact, she was thinking of going back to school and moving out of Georgia. She was currently working as a hairstylist and had a large clientele, some of which were celebrities. Between the sums of money she made from doing hair and Kevin's contributions, she was able to afford nice things, like the black Acura sitting out front.

As she talked about her life, I got the feeling she was tired of being the woman scorned. Kevin had hurt her to no end, and she was ready for a new life. He'd cheated on her on numerous occasions and even had a baby with some other woman. As she spoke about her life the look in her eyes grew sad and melancholy. I listened and hung on to every word she said. She spoke eloquently, but with a slight southern drawl.

I told her to be strong. She was a beautiful woman and didn't need any man to define her. For some reason, it was easy to talk to her. It was as if we had known each other all of our lives. I explained my situation with Jonathan and that I understood what she was going through. Although I was gay and she was straight, we realized we had so much in common, especially when it came to men. Before we knew it, it was 7:30 p.m., and Rashawn was busting through the door.

"Oh, no you didn't park in my spot, Miss Thang!" he said.

"Girl, I didn't see your name on that street. In fact, I could have sworn this was Tenth Street, not Rashawn Boulevard," Kim shot back. We all laughed. Kim was the kind of girl who wouldn't let Rashawn intimidate her. She gave it as good as she got it.

"Miss Tristan, how were your interviews?" Rashawn asked. I rolled my eyes to signify my feelings; Rashawn knew exactly what that meant. "Well, keep on trucking. It's only been one day," he said as he went into the kitchen.

"Oh yeah, that's what I been meaning to say," Kim perked up. "We got so caught up talking about the men in our lives that I forgot to tell you," she said. "I have a friend who is a receptionist at an event planning company. Maybe I can give her a call. I was talking to her the other day, and she said they are looking for new account managers."

"Oh, Kim, that would be great! That's just the kind of job I've been wanting," I said eagerly. I knew Kim was a friend worth having.

"Well, I won't make any promises, Trey, but I will call her tonight." We talked a little more, and Rashawn and I drank a lot more before Kim had to leave. She had to pick her son up. Luckily, he was at her mother's in-home daycare, so it was okay that she was running late. She left her scent of freshly picked flowers lingering in the air.

"Child, you sho love you some Kim," Rashawn said returning from the kitchen with two plates loaded down with fried chicken and greens, food left over from the party. Rashawn handed me a plate and plopped down in front of me. The chicken smelled really good, and I was famished. As I tore into the chicken, I realized I hadn't eaten since the breakfast Rashawn had cooked.

Rashawn and I talked for a short while. He told me about his new friend he'd recently met online, some trade boy with long dreads and a long piece to match. "I haven't seen it yet," Rashawn proclaimed, "but he's got a mean imprint in them jeans." Rashawn liked his men rough and tough. He usually only dealt with men who were secretly on the "down low." He claimed he didn't want anyone who queened out more than him.

After a couple of hours of chatting with Rashawn, I decided to head up to bed. I planned to soak in the tub and then crash on my big fluffy pillows. I ran my bathwater and turned my portable radio to V103. The water was hot and steamy and felt good on my skin. As I stood in the mirror stark naked, I marveled at my body. I was impressed with how my natural figure looked. I hardly worked out, and I ate just about whatever I wanted, yet I had washboard abs and a butt you could bounce a quarter off. The V shape torso was probably the sexiest part of my body. I smiled at myself. "God did a good job when he made me," I said to myself. I eased down into the water and lay my head back on the porcelain tub. I sighed deeply and let all my worries escape my mind. I closed my eyes and said a silent prayer.

> *"Lord, grant me the strength and patience*
> *to deal with any situation thrown upon me.*
> *I know it is your will that shall be done,*
> *and I give all the praise to you.*
> *I thank you for all the blessings bestowed upon me.*
> *And I ask that you show me favor upon finding a job.*
> *AMEN!*

As I prayed, calmness came over me, and I knew everything would be all right. That night I slept peacefully with sweet dreams of a bright future.

I awoke the next morning to the sound of my cell phone vibrating across the nightstand beside my bed. I looked at my digital clock; it was 5:30 a.m. Who could be calling me this early? I picked up the phone.

"Hello," I said with sleep still in my voice.

"Hey, Trey. It's Kim. Sorry to wake you."

"No problem," I said as I sat up in bed slightly annoyed. "Is everything okay?"

"Oh yeah, everything's good. I meant to call you last night. Remember my friend that works at the event planning company?"

"Yeah," I said.

"Well, she said you can stop by today around ten." *Wow*, I thought to myself, prayer works! "Her name is Yolanda. She's the administrative assistant. Let her know that you are there to see Yvette. She's the hiring manager." I jumped up and grabbed a pen and paper and began writing the information down. "The name of the company is OneStop Events, and they are located in the new building on the corner of Seventeenth and Peachtree." Kim gave me all the necessary details. As soon as we were done, I got off the phone, threw on my sweats, and went for a jog. I wanted to burn off the food from last night and clear my mind for the interview.

I arrived at 9:45 a.m. to Seventeenth and Peachtree. It was a pretty glass building that looked as if it had just been completed yesterday. The security guard on the main floor directed me to the tenth floor. On the elevator ride up, I made sure my suit was in order; I opted for the all black with blue shirt and tie. I had my resume in hand and a bright smile on my face. I must say I looked good.

The elevator opened up to an entry way. There was a high counter, and a woman in her late twenties sat behind it. The name plate identified her as Yolanda Brown, so I knew I was in the right place. Behind the receptionist was a large sign that read "OneStop Events" in gray lettering. To her right were two glass doors and to the left was a sitting area with a small table and magazines. I walked up to Yolanda to introduce myself. Before I could get a word out, she leaned forward and smiled, "You must be Tristan?"

Yolanda had a nice smile, her hair was pulled up into a French roll, and she had long manicured nails. She was a little plump but not overweight. I smiled back. "Yes ma'am, I'm supposed to meet with Yvette."

"Oh, I know, honey. You can have a seat." As I turned to walk toward the seating area, Yolanda mumbled. "Mmmh, Kim was right about you." I smiled to myself. Black folks can be so inappropriate. Seconds later Yolanda was on the phone. "Yeah, Yvette your ten o'clock is here . . . Okay . . . Okay . . . Thank you." She hung up the line "Yvette will be out in a moment. Make yourself comfortable. Would you like something to drink?" I declined and began flipping through one of the *Vibe* magazines on the table. It captured my attention because it had my girl, Mary J. Blige, on the cover. No sooner had I gotten through the first paragraph of her in-depth interview, a tall, thin, black woman wearing a pants suit with a short hair cut came walking through the glass doors.

She was semi-attractive. Her skin was an olive brown, and she wore wire rim glasses. She looked as if she was about her business. She walked straight up to me and extended her hand for me to shake. I stood quickly and gave her a firm hand shake. My mother always said you can tell a lot by a person's handshake. She escorted me through the double doors into a sprawling office. On one side of the office there were different conference rooms, on the other side individual offices, and in the middle large cubicles. As we headed to Yvette's office, I could have sworn I saw Faith Evans sitting in one of the conference rooms.

"Have a seat, Mr. Smith," Yvette instructed me once we reached her office. I sat in one of the plush seats facing her large, oak desk. I looked around her office. There was a large bookcase against the back wall with pictures of Yvette with various celebrities. She had an oversized bay window that looked out over the city. There were no signs of a family though. No pictures of kids or other family members. I took my seat and sat up straight.

"Well, Tristan, Kim speaks highly of you. May I see your résumé?" I handed her my freshly printed résumé. It included my internship as an account manager with Hewlett-Packard and my rank in the top ten percent of my class at the University of Nebraska. I had been included in the Who's Who of Collegiate Students nationwide and a part of just about every student organization available. "Nice résumé," Yvette said as she looked it over.

Yvette told me about the position; it was for an event planner/ account manager. The position was considered entry-level. OneStop

Events handled a lot of celebrity clients and big corporations around Atlanta. She explained their most recent account was Faith Evans and her album release party. I chuckled to myself when I realized that it was Faith Evans in that conference room. She asked me to tell her a little about myself.

Suddenly, I became nervous. I didn't want to screw this up, but it felt like I had a mouth full of cotton balls. I took several deep breaths before I started to talk. When I finally gathered myself, I took the time to sell myself. I explained how this job was exactly what I was looking for. I talked about how dedicated I was and how I would be willing to prove myself if only given a chance. By the end of the interview, I'd made it seem as if the company could not exist without me.

Yvette listened intently. I couldn't read her emotionless face as she sat quietly across from me. I was thinking the interview went well, but it was hard to tell. "Tristan, I'm very impressed," Yvette said as we wrapped up the interview. She reached out her hand for me to shake. *Oh no*, I thought, *here comes the brush off.* "Well, I'm definitely interested in hiring you," she continued. I was all set for disappointment. *Wait a minute. Did she say what I think she said?* "Of course I will have to talk it over with my boss, but I see no reason why we can't move forward."

Yvette was talking, but I was in another world. I couldn't believe what I was hearing. She was offering me a job on the spot. *Thank you, Lord,* I said to myself. "Of course we will have to run a background check, but I'll have Yolanda draw you up an offer letter." I couldn't believe my ears. "Mr. Smith . . . Mr. Smith." I snapped back to reality.

"Yes, ma'am," I said still in shock.

"So what do you think, Mr. Smith?"

"Well, I am truly excited," I said with a smile on my face so wide an ocean liner wouldn't have a problem pulling in. Yvette led me out of her office. As she escorted me to the front door, I floated on air. Just when I thought I couldn't get any happier, I saw him.

He was the finest man I had ever seen. As we passed by the men's restroom, he was walking out. He was wearing blue pleated slacks and a white button down with a striped tie. His arms and chest bulged through his shirt like an explosion. His slacks hugged his behind as if they were spray painted on. He had smooth, chocolate skin and a smile that pierced my soul. Low cut hair with deep waves topped him off. *Oh my! Who is this man from heaven?* I soon got my answer.

"Hey, Yvette," he said as he looked at me.

"Michael, hi. I'd like you to meet Tristan. He may be joining us." Michael reached for my hand, and I thought I wouldn't be able to move. I was paralyzed.

"Hi, Tristan," he said. Somehow I managed to shake his hand and mumble a meek hello. As our hands intertwined, I felt a shiver run through my body. It was as if he had reached into my soul and pulled it out.

"Michael is one of our senior account managers. If you are hired, you'll probably be working closely with him." Yvette just didn't know how happy she was making me. Michael said goodbye. I watched as he walked away and enjoyed every sway of his torso. His voice was so deep and defined, his look crisp and clean, yet I couldn't tell if he was batting for the girls or the boys. He appeared to be straight, but I couldn't be too sure. I guess I had some investigating to do. I left OneStop Events still walking on air. I decided I would have to do something nice for Kim because she had really come through for me.

~~~

"I'm so proud of you, baby. I knew if you gave it to God, He would work it out for you." My mother was just as happy as I was about my new job. It was Friday afternoon; Yvette had sent over my offer letter on Wednesday. I was more than pleased with the starting salary plus commission that they offered me. I was supposed to start Monday pending my drug test. Considering I had never done any sort of drugs in my entire life, I wasn't worried. I was lying across my bed with the windows opened enjoying the cool breeze and updating my mother on my first week in Atlanta. "Baby, I just can't believe how well things are working out for you so quickly."

"Yeah, Ma, I can't believe it either. I keep waiting for something horrible to happen, God forbid," I said. "How's Corey doing?" I hadn't spoken to him since I'd left Nebraska.

"He's fine, baby. You know Trina is giving him the blues because he's about to have the new baby." Trina was Corey's first baby momma who he was no longer with. He had a new baby on the way by a girl named Nisi. I could never keep track of Corey's girlfriends.

I looked at the clock; it read 4:30 p.m. I needed to start getting ready. I'd purchased two tickets to Beyonce's concert at the Phillips Arena. I decided I would take Kim out as a thank you for the hook up on the job. She was picking me up at six. We wanted to get there early. "Well, Ma, I gotta go. You know I'm going to see Beyonce tonight."

"Oh, yeah, I forgot. You tell that Beyonce I really enjoy her, but she got to cover up a little more."

I laughed at my mother; it was funny how she thought I was going to be talking to Beyonce personally. "Okay, Momma, I love you, and I'll call you later. Tell Corey I love him too."

"Bye, baby," my mother said as she hung up. I sat there for a moment and looked at the phone. I really loved my mother, and I wished she were here with me. I guess our phone calls would have to suffice.

I hung up the phone and jumped into the shower. I picked out some linen pants and a V neck shirt that accented my arms and chest; it made them appear larger than they actually were. I pushed back my curly hair. I had a head of thick, curly hair that I would pick out into an afro or, like today, put a little product in it and comb it back. I checked myself out in the mirror; I looked like I'd just stepped off the plane from Jamaica. To top it off, my light skin had a bronzy tan. It wasn't long before Kim was at the door. I gave myself one more glance over before I skipped down the stairs excited about our evening out with Beyonce.

Kim looked fabulous as ever. Her hair was bone straight as if she had flat ironed each strand individually. She wore a pair of tight fitting jeans that flared at the bottom with stiletto heels. Her top was a shimmer gold that reflected the light and cast a glow over her face. We both looked like celebrities.

The concert was off the chain. Kim and I sang along with the diva on every song. We screamed so loud I thought I wouldn't be able to speak again. A few times I even thought I caught eye contact with her. By the end of the concert, Kim and I were worn out. We cut out of there and headed to Waffle House for a late dinner and to wind down.

"Oh my God, Trey! That was so much fun," Kim said as she took a bite of her pecan waffle. "Thank you so much."

"No problem," I said. "It was the least I could do considering you got me such a wonderful job."

"I didn't get you the job. I just gave you the contact. Yolanda told me that Yvette was real impressed with your interview."

I blushed. "Oh by the way, who is that Michael guy? He is fine!" I said.

"Yeah, he is good looking. I've met him a couple of times," Kim replied.

"What's his story?" I asked eager to get the dirt.

Kim looked at me and smiled. "Oh, Trey, do you have a little crush?" We both laughed. Kim said she didn't know much about Michael. She had only met him when going to visit Yolanda at work. After we finished eating, Kim dropped me off at home. She had to hurry and pick up her son from his father's house. She didn't like to leave him over there for too long. We said our goodbyes, and she drove off.

Saturday came and went. I spent most of the day doing research on my new job. I looked on the internet and found articles. OneStop Events was an up and coming company that grossed in the millions last year. They did everything from planning weddings and social events to big celebrity parties. Their clients included the Coca-Cola Company, Heineken, and celebrities like Faith Evans and Usher. They even did charity events. I was excited to be joining a company with such potential. After doing my research, I went into my closet to pick out my outfit for Monday. I decided to go with a pair of gray slacks and a pastel blue button down with a matching tie. Later, I joined Rashawn in front of the television for dinner and a movie.

We hadn't seen much of each other; he had been spending time with his new friend whom he hadn't introduced to me yet. We watched TV together on the couch until we both were asleep. I woke up the next morning to the sound of Yolanda Adams blaring from the downstairs stereo. I was in my bed, but I didn't remember how I got there. One too many Long Island Iced Teas thanks to Rashawn. I looked at my clock—9:30 a.m. Rashawn was singing along to the music as he got dressed. My head was pounding, but I realized it was Sunday. That meant the whole gang was getting together for church. I hopped in the shower, got dressed, and met Rashawn downstairs.

"Well, don't you look like Easter, gurl," Rashawn said as he grabbed my hand and twirled me around. My headache had worn off thanks to the long, hot shower. We giggled and headed out the front door.

The church we attended was called New Beginning Baptist Church. Located in Decatur, it wasn't a mega church, but it wasn't far from it. Bishop Eddie Morton was the pastor. Rashawn and I arrived just as the choir was starting to rock. We spotted Eric and Tyler seated a few rows back from the front. We took our seats; Eric managed to save a spot for me right next to him. Just as we sat down Kim walked in with her son, Jamal. Jamal was the cutest little boy. He had on a blue suit with a bow tie and a smile that stretched from here to eternity. Kim sat on the other side of me; she introduced me to her son.

"Nice to meet you," Jamal said with a proper southern accent.

I smiled. "Nice to meet you too, Jamal."

As the choir sang, we all shouted and hollered. From time to time, we would jump out our seats and raise our hands to the sky. When the Bishop came out, we all took our seats and listened to his sermon about patience and dealing with our daily struggles. He said to pray and ask God to give you patience to deal with any situation you are in. By the end of the service, I felt renewed and cleansed.

After church we headed to Tyler's apartment for brunch, part of the weekly tradition. Tyler lived in Marietta. It was a little drive out to his place, but he had already cooked the meal. He'd prepared shrimp cocktail, pasta salad, grilled chicken breast, and broccoli casserole. Everything was delicious. "Boy, Tyler, I didn't know you could throw down like this!" I said as I piled food onto my plate.

"Child, I don't look like this for nothing," he said rubbing his protruding belly. We all laughed. I took a seat on the sofa in the living room. I was hoping Kim would sit next to me, but Eric beat her to it.

"So how's your first week in Atlanta?" Eric asked sitting so close to me I thought he was going to end up in my lap!

"It's going pretty well," I said trying to move over, but with no luck. I was already on the end of the sofa.

"Child, move your tail over, Miss Eric! Tristan is not thinking 'bout you," Rashawn said saving the day.

Eric rolled his eyes at Rashawn. "You're just mad 'cause I'm not sitting next to you."

"Gurl, please, you know I ain't got no time for no wanna be man. I needs me a real man." Rashawn took a bite of his food. Kim made

Jamal a plate and got him situated in the kitchen. She knew from previous brunches that the conversation could get a little R-rated, so she wanted to make sure that he was out of earshot. Once he was settled, she came and joined the group.

"So what's the tea, Miss Kim? You sho have been kickin' it with Tristan a lot this week," Rashawn said between bites.

Kim smiled at me. "Well, you know he just has so much class." I laughed at that comment. "I think I finally got rid of Kevin though," Kim said. "I met a new guy a couple of weeks ago, and Kevin hasn't been bothering me as much."

We were all ears listening. "Gurl, you done met somebody, and you ain't share that with the club!" Rashawn blurted out.

"Shut up, Rashawn, and let her tell the story," Tyler said.

"Well, I didn't want to get ahead of myself. Plus, we are just friends. We're not serious yet," Kim said with a smile. It was the kind of smile that showed there was more to the story.

"What's his name?" Rashawn was about ready to jump out his seat.

"His name is Brandon, and he works as an electrician. We met when he came into the shop to get a haircut." Kim told us how they had been on a couple of dates, and he seemed really nice.

"Skip the pleasantries. What does he look like?" Rashawn had no class. "I mean is he fine? He got a big tool? Come on, Miss Thang! Don't hold back on us now." I reached over and smacked Rashawn.

"Well, he is good looking, and I don't know what's between his legs just yet. I'm not that kind of girl," Kim said blushing.

"Child, please, if he looks good enough, you'll be that kind of girl." Rashawn said. We all fell out laughing.

We spent the rest of the day laughing and gossiping. I had to tell Eric more than once to keep his hands to himself. As it got late, Kim was the first to leave since she had to get Jamal home. That was the beauty of not having kids; you didn't have to worry about someone else all the time. But I could tell by how Kim treated Jamal that she didn't mind at all. Rashawn and I hung around a little longer, until Rashawn got a phone call from his secret boyfriend and we had to leave as well. "See you all next week at my place," Rashawn said as he dragged me out the front door.

When we got home, we had a visitor sitting on our front stoop. "Oh no he didn't just show up at my house!" Rashawn said as he parked in his usual spot next to my Neon. "I told him I would call when I got home," Rashawn's face was so pinched up. I could tell he was not happy. I figured this must be the secret boyfriend Rashawn was keeping from everyone.

As we got out the car and walked towards the front door, the mystery man stood up. He looked as if he had a piece between his legs as long as his arm. He was tall and had long dreads that he wore balled up like a Rastafarian. He had on a pair of Timbs and some baggy jeans. His skin was smooth and flawless, the color of cocoa butter. He chewed a toothpick and smelled like marijuana.

"What are you doing here?" Rashawn said walking past him and opening the front door.

"I wanted to see you, baby," he replied in a deep baritone voice, so deep it gave me chills. I walked in past the two of them, and he stared at me as if wondering who I was.

"Oh, Tristan, this is Eli . . . Eli, this is Tristan." Rashawn was being very rude.

"Nice to meet you," I said extending my hand to shake his. He shook my hand but never looked me in the eyes. He only glared at my behind. I was feeling uncomfortable, so I took my hand back and headed to my room, leaving Rashawn and Eli to argue alone. When I got to my room, I shut the door, turned on some soft music, and climbed into bed. I had a big day ahead of me. I was expected to be at work by eight. I fell asleep with the sounds of V103's Joyce Litell playing slow jams in my ear.

CHAPTER 2

Tristan

*M*onday morning was a big day. I awoke at 6:30 a.m., showered, and went downstairs for breakfast. I was startled by Eli already in the kitchen making a bowl of cereal. "Oh! I'm sorry. I didn't know anyone was in here," I said. I had on a pair of boxers and a white T-shirt. I felt naked especially considering how he just stared at me. "Where's Rashawn?" I said.

"Oh, he still sleepin', kid. You know I puts it down, and da honeys don't be wantin' to get up."

I rolled my eyes. Why couldn't black folks speak proper English? I went back upstairs. I'd had enough of his foolishness. I would just have to grab something to eat on the way to work. I dressed and left out the house, leaving Eli on the couch eating his cereal and watching cartoons.

I made my way through the maze of downtown Atlanta. It was such a culture shock coming from my humble beginnings in Omaha to the hustle and bustle of Atlanta. The most traffic I'd endured in

Omaha was the line to get into Time Out, a local chicken joint in the heart of north Omaha.

I arrived at 7:40 a.m., twenty minutes early. Yolanda was not at the front desk, and it appeared to be dark in the office. I went through the double glass doors. There were a few people in the office, most were in line for coffee. The first person to greet me was Michael himself. "Hey, Tristan, good morning," he said with his signature bright smile. I knew it was going to be hard to focus on work with this man beaming at me all day.

"Good morning, Michael," I said a little nervous. "I know I'm a little early but . . ."

Michael cut me off. "No problem, bud. I figured you would be in early. That's why I came in." I smiled; he'd come in just for me. "Yeah, Yvette usually gets in around eight, and I usually get here around nine, but it's cool. Let me show you around."

Michael took me on a tour of the office. He showed me my cubicle which was directly beside his. He introduced me to a couple of other account managers. There was Tammy, whose cubicle was in front of mine. She was the one working on the Faith Evans's event. Then there was Kyle. He was on the other side of my cubicle. Kyle was one of the few Caucasians that worked in the office.

As eight o'clock approached, I met some other coworkers. Victor was the CEO; he was the one who had given approval to hire me. "Tristan, nice to meet you," he said in a hearty voice. "I'm counting on you, so don't let me down."

I smiled. "I promise I won't," I replied. Victor was an older black man with salt and pepper in his beard and mustache; however, he looked very nice for his age. Just as we were walking out of Victor's office, Yvette was walking up.

"Hello, Tristan, good morning and welcome to OneStop Events." We exchanged pleasantries. "I hope Michael is treating you well," she said as she winked at Michael.

"Oh, he is," I said.

"So, are you ready to get started?" Yvette said. I nodded as I followed her, eager to begin the day.

That morning I went through a crash course on the history of the company with Yvette. She went over all the policies and what was expected of me. I was on a ninety-day probationary period where my performance would be monitored to determine if I was a good fit for the company. The best part of the job was the American Express business card that I would be issued within thirty days. It was supposed to cover any travel, lodging, or food expenses I incurred while working. As long as I turned in receipts, I was okay.

Yvette had me watch a couple of videos on sexual harassment in the workplace, ethics, and money management. The money management video talked about using the American Express card wisely. Just when I thought I was going to lapse into a coma, Yvette came back into the conference room where I was watching the videos. "Lunch time," she said. I looked at the wall clock. It read twelve o'clock. Good cause I needed a change, and my stomach was starting to sound like a grizzly bear. Yvette and Michael decided to take me to lunch.

We went to Einstein's, a place off of Juniper Street downtown. We ate outside on the patio. "So," Yvette started, "I hope I didn't bore you to death with the videos."

"No, I can handle it," I said munching on my pecan chicken salad.

"Well, I hope you can handle it. I took a risk on you, but I have a feeling you will do wonderful," she said.

"Yeah, I'm sure you'll do fine. The key is doing whatever it takes to make the client happy," Michael chimed in. *God, he's gorgeous*, I thought to myself. I couldn't take my eyes off of him. He had a certain sparkle in his eyes that was enchanting. Yvette and Michael talked about the different accounts they had and how to be successful with the company. It was determined I would shadow Michael for a little while, and of course I had no objections to that. We talked and laughed, and before we knew it, an hour and a half had passed. Yvette paid our bill, and we headed back to the office.

I spent the rest of the afternoon setting up my cubicle. It was my first real job, and I was excited to start making it a home. I created a voicemail greeting on my phone and arranged things on my desk. I also got to know a few coworkers. The highlight of the day was when Tammy came into my cube.

Tammy was a fly girl at heart. Although she had on a suit, she still wore her bamboo earrings and had long nails. "Hey, Tristan," she said peeking into my cubicle with her flat iron looking fresh to death.

"Yes, Tammy," I said. I was reading one of the many manuals that lay in front of me.

"I have someone for you to meet," Tammy had a big smile on her face. I got out my chair and followed her to a conference room. There she was, Ms. Faith Evans herself. She looked gorgeous. She had her hair pulled back into a ponytail, and she had on a pair of designer glasses. "Faith, this is one of our new associates, Tristan Smith." Tammy introduced us.

"Hey, Tristan, you're cute," she said with her raspy voice. I couldn't believe it. I grew up jamming to her music and here she was at arm's length.

"Hi, Miss Evans," I stammered. I was blushing all over the place.

"Are you coming to my album release party? You know Miss Tammy has been working her butt off to get this party going."

"Of course, Miss Evans. I wouldn't miss it for the world," I said, my eyes glowing with excitement.

"Well good, but you can call me Faith, honey. I ain't no old lady." We laughed. "Tammy, I'm going to send my agent over to cut you that final check, and I guess I'll see you Friday night, and you too, Tristan."

"Okay," I said star-struck. Tammy escorted Faith to the front door, and I went back to my cubicle. Wow, my first day on the job, and I was already going to a celebrity party!

~~~

"Mom, it was wonderful. The people were nice, and I'm even going to a celebrity party this Friday." I was home lying across my bed. I called my mother as soon as I walked into the house. I was so excited about my first day at work.

"Well, baby that's good. Just make sure you don't get involved with any drugs. You know those big celebrity parties tend to have drugs and alcohol." My mother was the incessant worrier. I explained to her that it was an album release party and that Faith was going for a new image, so they were having the party at the local skating rink, Cascade Skates. They were inviting some high school students who had won tickets off a local radio show, so it really wasn't that kind of party, although a couple of heavy hitters were going to be there, like Jermaine Dupree and Monica. Also Frank Ski from V103 was going to deejay. I figured I would take this time to shadow Tammy, so I would be doing more working than partying. My mother was happy for me. She wished me luck and said she would pray for me like always. Thus was the end of my first Monday.

The rest of the week was filled with events and presentations. Michael had to give a presentation on his next event. He was planning a party for a web design company's launch date. The whole office attended a Heineken event where we passed out free T-shirts to the first 100 people. I was also able to sit in on a couple of meetings with Yvette and Victor. There really was no official training. I was just supposed to catch on. The office moved at a fast pace. Every morning there was a staff meeting where the account managers updated everyone on what they were working on. This was the time where new events were delegated. Some were high profile while others were just standard events.

By Thursday I had kind of gotten used to the flow of things. I stayed late with Tammy that evening. She was putting together gift bags for the Faith Evans's event; we were stuffing posters and CDs in the gift bags. We were just wrapping up around 6:30 p.m. when my cell phone rang. "Sorry, Tammy, let me take this call," I said as I walked out of the conference room to answer my phone.

The display read Eric. I rolled my eyes before answering, "Hello," I said not at all enthused.

"Hey, Tristan, it's Eric."

"I know who it is," I said.

"Oh really? So you must like the sound of my voice," he replied. I was getting tired of Eric's advances. I really was not into him. He was attractive, but I saw him more as a friend.

"What's up, Eric?" I said ignoring his come-ons.

"Nothing. I was just wondering if you wanted to go out with me and Tyler."

"Where to?" I said trying to be short with him.

"Well, we usually go to Bulldogs on Thursday nights." Bulldogs was a little bar located right on Peachtree not far from my job. I had been there before when I came down for spring break. It was one of those places where the men had only one thing on their minds. Most of the men walked around with their shirts off showing their bodies. Some were in shape and others weren't, but that didn't stop them from pulling it all off. Then there were the old men walking around knowing they needed to be at home in bed. Since the club sat right on Peachtree, you hardly ever got the closeted boys. Most of the men that frequented Bulldogs were out and proud of it. Since I was having such a good week and Tyler was going as well, I decided I would go.

"Okay, Eric. I'll go. Do you want me to meet you there?"

"No, I was thinking Tyler and I could swing by your place, and you could ride with us." I sighed I really didn't want to ride with Eric; I liked to be in control of when I left the club. Sometimes I liked to cut out early, but for some reason I gave in. "Great!" Eric replied. "We'll be there by eleven." I left the office shortly after my conversation with Eric. Tammy was just wrapping up, and she didn't need any more help.

When I got home, I found Eli in the living room with his feet propped up on the table as he flicked through the channels. I rolled my eyes; it was as if he was my roommate and not Rashawn. "Hey, kid," Eli said.

"Where's Rashawn?" I said ignoring the stares he gave me. "He's upstairs. Why you be givin' me so much attitude, man? What I do to you?" He looked me up and down like he wanted to jump my bones. I ignored him and ran up the stairs. I found Rashawn in his room getting dressed. The covers on his bed were freshly messed up, so I was sure they had just finished doing the do.

"Hey, gurl," Rashawn said zipping his pants up.

"Hey, Rashawn, how are you?"

"I'm good. Just got some good lovin' from my man." That was too much information I thought to myself.

"Rashawn, look you need . . ." I was just about to tell Rashawn to be careful with Eli because I didn't trust him, but Rashawn cut me off.

"Gurl, I got to go. Eli and I are going to get something to eat; you know I can't keep my man waiting." With that Rashawn was gone. He ran down the stairs, and a few seconds later, I heard the front door shut.

I didn't understand what Rashawn saw in Eli. Rashawn was talented and smart; he had a lot going for himself. The only thing Eli seemed to have was good sex. It was hard to just sit back and watch a friend go down a path that was destined for destruction. I shook it off though. Rashawn was a grown man, and I'm sure he knew what he was doing. Or did he?

Eric and Tyler pulled up at exactly eleven o'clock. We decided to have a few drinks at the house before we went out. "Hey, Tristan," Tyler said as I opened the door to let them in. Tyler was always in a good mood. "Don't you look nice," he said to me admiring my outfit. I had on a pair of jeans that hugged my behind in just the right way. I wore a T-shirt that read "Get N 2 It" across the front. The sleeves hugged my arms and showed off my muscles. I also wore a pair of Nike tennis shoes, something I hardly ever wore. Eric couldn't take his eyes off me as I made each of us a drink.

"You ready to party, child?" Tyler said bouncing around like he was slap happy.

"Boy, calm your big self down," Eric frowned at Tyler. It was funny to think that Eric and Tyler were such good friends. They were like night and day and were always fussing with each other, but I guess that's what good friends do. I jumped up and started dancing with Tyler.

"He's just having fun, Eric," I said to him. We drank and talked for about thirty minutes. When my buzz was just right, we headed to the club.

Tyler was the designated driver so the drink at the house was the only one he was having. But I was feeling good, so as soon as we got in the club, I headed straight to the bar. The club was packed. It was as if it was Labor Day weekend or MLK Day, holidays when all the boys came out. I had to bump and push my way to the bar. Once I got my drink, I joined Tyler and Eric on the dance floor.

The music pumped so loudly that it felt like my eardrums would burst. My heartbeat danced along with the music. Eric took this opportunity to get close to me. He eased behind me and put his hands on my waist. I guess it was the liquor or the good music, but I let him go with it. We grinded on each other to no end. At one point,

I could feel his manhood poking through his pants. That's when I knew it was time to stop.

"I'm thirsty!" I yelled into Eric's ear trying to be heard over the loud music. "I'm going to get another drink." I left Eric standing there with his piece at full attention. I laughed to myself while thinking, *I'm such a tease.* I made my way to the patio to catch some fresh air. On my way out, I grabbed a bottle of water.

As I stood in the breeze, I drank the water as if it was the last ounce of water on the face of the earth. It felt so good going down my throat. I leaned up against a tree and let the night air take me away. As I stood there relaxing, oblivious to my surroundings, I noticed out the corner of my eye a man staring at me. I glanced back to make sure. Yep, he was looking. He stood back in the corner of the patio as if lurking in the shadow. He was about six feet tall, nice build, and beautiful eyes. He wore blue jeans and Timberlands with an oversized T-shirt. He looked as if he didn't belong in this establishment. As I peered out the corner of my eyes, careful not to let him see me looking, I noticed him walking toward me. Oh my goodness! Was he coming to talk? What was I going to say? I was so not ready for this. Wait . . . wait . . . here he comes . . .

"Hello, how are you?" Before I knew it, he was before me. His voice was a soft and mellow yet deep voice that had an air of confidence.

I looked up at him. "Um, are you talking to me?" I stammered. *What a dumb response*, I thought to myself as soon as I'd said it.

He smiled. "Um, yeah. I don't see anyone else standing over here," he replied.

"Oh, hi. How are you?" I said as nervous as ever.

"Well, I wanted to come speak because I know you saw me staring at you, and I didn't want you to think I was some freak or something." He talked as if he was so sure of himself. I liked that.

"Oh, I didn't notice you looking," I lied.

"Well, anyways, my name is BJ," he said ignoring my lie.

"I'm Tristan," I answered back extending my hand for him to shake. His grip was firm and in control.

"Tristan, you look like you were out there working it out."

"What do you mean?" He pointed to the dance floor. "Oh yeah, I was just enjoying myself with my friends," I said.

He stood so close to me I could smell his cologne. It smelled like Burberry, one of my favorites. As the breeze from the night air blew, I got lost in this man's eyes. They were a deep gray. As he talked to me, I inhaled his scent. He told me he had seen me when I first walked in. He said he liked how it seemed as if I was having fun from the time I hit the front door. He told me he was not a regular at Bulldogs, and he rarely picked guys up at the bar. Although that was what most of the men said when they were trying to take you home, for some reason I believed him. Before the night ended, we exchanged numbers. I gave him my cell number, and he gave me his pager number. He said that was the fastest way to reach him. Before I knew it, it was three o'clock, and the lights were coming on in the club. BJ whispered goodbye in my ear, his lips lightly brushing against my cheek, and then he left.

Just as he was leaving Eric and Tyler came walking up. "Honey, we saw that fine piece of man you were talking to," Tyler said with a grin on his face. Eric rolled his eyes. "He was cute, child. Who was that?" Tyler grabbed my arm and dragged me outside. Eric followed behind looking like a lost puppy.

"He was just some boy that thought I was cute," I said as we walked to the car.

"Well, honey, did you get his number?" Tyler pressed.

"Yeah, we exchanged numbers," I left out the part that I only got his pager number. Eric let out a loud sigh; Tyler turned around and laughed at him.

"Child, Eric, pick up yo lip! You know there ain't nothing you and Ms. Tristan can do. Y'all both lil ladies." I laughed. Tyler was right about that. Still yet, I felt bad.

As we pulled up to my place, I got out the car and leaned in the passenger side window. I planted a big kiss on Eric's cheek. "I'm sorry, Eric." I said.

He looked at me and smiled. "It's okay. At least I got to rub on dem cakes while we danced." We laughed, and I said goodbye. I ran in the house jumped in the shower and went to sleep. I had to be at work by nine.

Kim

Kim was tired of her life. She had a no good baby daddy and a dead end job. She was over doing hair, standing on her feet for hours at a time pretending that she cared about what her clients were talking about. She was sick of trying to make the ghetto chick from around the block look like Beyonce. I mean damn! She wasn't a miracle worker. This particular day she was in no mood to deal with pitiful customers and their whiny stories about baby daddy drama, rent problems, and sexual frustrations. Hell, she had those same problems. She might as well have had a degree in psychology; at least then she would be making more money. Today was particularly bad because she was running late. She had a 9:30 a.m. client coming in, it was already nine o'clock, and Jamal didn't want to get ready for daycare.

"Jamal, come on, honey. Mommy has to go to work." She threw on her work shoes; they were a comfortable pair of sneakers that she could stand in for long stretches. Just as she and Jamal were heading to the car, Jamal's dad, Kevin, pulled up. Kim rolled her eyes. What was he doing there so early in the morning?

Kevin drove a 1976 Chevy Impala. His rims and speakers probably cost more than the car itself. He had gold in his mouth, and his hair was freshly braided back in cornrows. He spoke with a thick southern accent. "Yo, Kim! Gurl, come here! I wanna talk to you," he yelled out the car window.

"Hi, daddy!" Jamal said.

"Hey, boy! Come give daddy a hug."

Kim did not have time for this. "Look, Kevin, I have to go! What do you want?" She was irritated.

"Gurl, why you got to wear the tightest jeans to work?" he said looking Kim up and down.

Kim ignored his comment. "Can you take Jamal to my mother's? I'm running late." Jamal ran to the passenger side door excited to be going with his daddy.

"Yo, Kim, who dis new kat you kickin' it wit? My boy, Reggie, told me he saw you at some restaurant wit a nigga dat he ain't know?"

Kim knew exactly who he was talking about. She had gone out with Brandon the other day, and Reggie, one of Kevin's ghetto friends, was out with an equally ghetto girl. Kim thought about hiding or going to another restaurant, but she was grown, and she and Kevin were not together. "Look, Kevin, just drop Jamal off. I ain't got time for this. Bye, Jamal. Love you, baby." Kim blew her son a kiss.

"Bye, mommy," Jamal said. Kim hopped in her car and sped off leaving Kevin there to ponder who her new friend was.

Kim met Kevin in high school. She was a freshman, and he was a sophomore. Back then he had everything going for himself. He was a star basketball player who made decent grades. But when his older brother got released from jail, Kevin started hanging around him and his friends. Kevin began to sell drugs, and he became addicted to money. Kim had to admit that she liked all the expensive things Kevin would bring home to her, but his attention to school started slacking. Kevin dropped off the basketball team and barely graduated from high school. He only managed to pass his classes with the help of Kim. Kim loved him for a long time. In fact, she still had love for him. He had just hurt her too much for her to go back to him. He was a good father, however.

Kevin spent lots of time with Jamal. Kim knew he would never do anything to hurt their son. One day in the middle of the night Kevin came home drunk. He looked as if he had been in a fight. Jamal was only about two years old at the time. "Kevin, what's wrong? What happened?!?!" Kim screamed at him. All he kept saying was he would kill anyone who tried to mess with his son. He said it repeatedly. Later, he gave Kim the key to a safety deposit box that was filled with money. She was instructed to not touch the money unless something happened to him. That money was supposed to take care of Jamal. I guess he didn't believe in insurance policies. Kim always kept the key close to her. She never knew what might happen. At any rate, she didn't have time for Kevin's mess . . . especially not today.

Kim got to the hair salon a little past 9:30 a.m. Her client was sitting there waiting with an irritated look on her face. "I'm sorry, Ms. Gladys. I'll be ready in a minute."

"You know I have to get to work, honey," her client replied. That was the beginning of her day. As Kim did head after head she dreamt of owning her own shop and not having to do hair at all. She had a plan in the works. She had a little money saved, but she was still a ways off. By four that afternoon, she had made $600. She was tired and ready to go home.

Just when she thought she had enough, she got a pleasant surprise. The door opened up to the shop and a flower delivery man walked in. He was carrying two dozen roses. "Is there a Kim Taylor here?" the delivery man yelled over the loud music and chattering women. Everyone stopped in their place and looked toward him. Kim was all smiles. Every woman in the shop was envious of Kim at that moment. Who wouldn't want to get roses at work?

"I'm Kim," she said practically skipping up to the delivery man.

"I have a delivery for you from a Brandon Jackson," he handed her the flowers and sort of stood there. Kim reached in her apron and pulled out a five dollar bill and handed it to him. The delivery man grabbed the money and hurried out the shop. Kim read the card. *"Beautiful flowers for a beautiful woman."* That was all of the card she read, and that was all she needed to read. Kim felt good. Finally, she had met someone who knew how to make a woman feel special! Kim finished with her last client and headed out the shop feeling much better than when she arrived.

She picked up Jamal from her mother's daycare, and they headed home together. She had called Brandon earlier that day and offered to cook dinner for him. She usually didn't like bringing men around her son this early in the game, but Brandon was different. She trusted him.

She arrived home around 6:45 p.m. She was going to make her favorite dish, spaghetti. It was quick, easy, and left time for her to get ready before Brandon showed up. As the food simmered on the stove, Kim hopped in the shower. After she showered, she lotioned her body with an expensive body crème and slipped on her favorite silk lace panties and matching bra. Kim took a moment to admire her body in the mirror. She was thick in all the right places. But one too many burgers and Kim had the potential of being considered fat. Luckily, she exercised and watched what she ate so she didn't have to worry about that.

Kim fed Jamal in the kitchen before Brandon arrived. Jamal was the man of her house, so he always ate first. After his dinner, she gave him a kiss on his forehead and shut his bedroom door.

Just as she was lighting the candles in the living room, the doorbell rang. Kim gave herself one last glance over. She had decided to wear a sundress that was long and flowy. When she answered the door, Brandon stood in the doorway looking sexy as ever. He smelled of a soft cologne. She couldn't quite make out the scent, but she was sure she had smelled it before. Probably from Kevin.

He loved drowning himself in a variety of colognes. Brandon gently bent down and kissed Kim on the lips. It was a soft, sweet kiss that made her feel tingly inside.

Once inside the apartment, they sat next to each other on the sofa, sipped wine, and talked. Brandon had a way of listening to Kim that made her feel important, like what she said really mattered. After a hearty plate of pasta and more wine, they ended up on the balcony enjoying the night air. Brandon sat close to Kim, so close that Kim could feel his heart beat. Before she knew it, they were in her room.

Brandon began kissing Kim all over her body, taking his time to savor every inch of her. Kim trembled with nervousness as Brandon ran his fingers across the small of her back. They looked each other in the eyes. Brandon could tell Kim wasn't ready for this much intimacy. He pulled her close to him and squeezed. He hugged her tight as she laid her head on his chest. They lay together in the bed, Brandon holding her tight, and they slept peacefully. The next morning Kim awoke, and Brandon was gone. There was a note on her night table.

> *Kim, thank you for a wonderful night.*
> *I look forward to spending more time with you.*
> *Sorry I took off, but I had to go to work.*
> *Until next time . . . Brandon*

Kim smiled to herself. Had she finally found the man she'd been looking for?

CHAPTER 3

Tristan

J went to work Friday morning a little hung over, but it was okay because it was Faith Evans's album release party, and I was on the guest list! I couldn't get to work fast enough. The morning ran smoothly. I was assigned to help Michael on his next event, which was taking place the following week. Yvette let me sit in on a conference call, and I helped Tammy finish up some last minute details for the party.

At lunch, Michael and I decided to go shopping for something to wear that night. I was pleased when he asked me to join him. I needed something to wear, and I definitely wanted to spend time with him. Michael was hard to read though. All the girls in the office loved him, yet he didn't give them the time of day. Yolanda, the office admin and designated know-it-all (she knew everybody's business), said he didn't have a girlfriend or a boyfriend for that matter, so she didn't know whose team he was batting for. Everything about him screamed straight man, but of course I had my dreams.

We decided to go to Lenox Square Mall. It was a bright sunny day, and the mall was packed. Michael and I weaved in and out of the crowd going from one store to the next. We ended up in Bloomingdale's. I had no idea how I was supposed to dress for this kind of event, so I looked to Michael for guidance. "Just be yourself, shorty," he said. My heart skipped a beat when he called me shorty.

"That's the problem, Michael. I don't really know what being myself is." I let myself be a little vulnerable; Michael was the kind of guy who was so sure of himself that it was easy to just let go around him.

He walked over to a rack of slacks and held a pair up against his toned body. "What do you think?" he asked. I smiled and gave him my approval. I was nervous around Michael. I needed to loosen up. As we shopped, we talked about a variety of things. Michael was from Detroit and a few years older than me. He came to Atlanta for school and graduated from Morehouse College.

I tried on a pair of wide leg slacks with a Sean John sport jacket. It looked really hip on me. "Yo, Tristan, that outfit is tight. You should get it," Michael said. I looked at the price tag of the jacket, $250. I guess good taste wasn't cheap. Michael settled on a pair of fitted Seven Jeans and a V-neck black knit shirt. He looked gorgeous in the simple denim and T-shirt look. We walked out of Bloomingdale's with our bags and headed toward the food court to grab a bite to eat.

I ended up spending more money than expected at Bloomingdale's, so lunch would have to be cheap. As we stood in line at Chick-fil-A, I heard someone calling my name. "Tristan! Hey, Tristan!" To my surprise it was Rashawn. He came running up to me all smiles. He was dressed in his usual flashy gear. Extra tight slacks, a pink T-shirt that said "Flaming" across the front with his dreads pulled into a ponytail. Although it screamed gay, Rashawn still looked good. Rashawn could wear a plastic bag and make it look good. "Gurl, what are you doin' here?" he said waving his hands in the air.

G. L. Johnson

I looked at Michael; he had a "oh my God" look on his face. I was immediately embarrassed. "Hey, Rashawn," I said. Rashawn looked at the bags in my hand then looked at Michael.

"Is this the fine boy from last night? You know Tyler called and gave me the tea, honey," Rashawn started laughing, but I wasn't. I was so embarrassed my face had turned a beet red. "Honey, what's wrong? Cat got yo tongue? Child, he fine for real, gurl." Sometimes Rashawn did not know how to shut up.

"Um, I'm Michael, Tristan's coworker," Michael extended his hand to shake Rashawn's.

Rashawn's eyes widened and his mouth formed a perfect O but nothing came out. Now it was his turn to be embarrassed. "Oh, I'm sorry. I'm Rashawn, Tristan's roommate; just forget everything I just said." *I could just slap him,* I thought to myself. "Tristan, I'll see you at the house," Rashawn said backing away.

"Yeah," I said, "I'll see you there, big mouth." Rashawn walked off leaving me there to face Michael. I turned to look at him. I was certain Michael would never hang with me again. "I'm sorry, Michael," I said with my head down.

"What are you sorry for? You didn't do anything," Michael started to order his food.

"I mean I know Rashawn might have made you feel uncomfortable," I said.

"Nawl, it's cool. I have a couple of gay friends back in Detroit, and my uncle is gay. It's not a big deal. He was loud though," Michael said laughing.

I ordered my food. "Well, you know . . ." I stammered. For some reason I was nervous to say I was gay to Michael. I mean I'm sure he'd figured it out, but I was nervous to say it aloud. Kind of like when I first told my mother. I knew that she knew, but I was just scared to say it. "Um, well, I'm gay also, Michael."

Michael looked at me and laughed. Not the response I was hoping for. "Kid, it's cool. I said it before, I'm not a caveman. It's not a problem. We are cool."

"So you don't mind?" I asked.

"Well, Tristan, we work together, so I really don't have a choice. Besides you are good people. I could tell that when I first met you. Seriously, kid, you have got to lighten up a bit." We both laughed as we carried our trays to a table to eat.

Everyone cut out early from the office on Friday. I was headed home to get ready for the party, but before doing so, I had to cuss out Rashawn. When I got home I found Rashawn in the kitchen cooking up some concoction. I sat my bags on the floor and went into the kitchen. "Rashawn, I could just wring your neck!" I said.

"I'm sorry, gurl. I just thought that was the same boy from last night. I mean Tyler went on and on about how you met some fine piece of trade," Rashawn said in a matter of fact manner.

"Well, you could have approached us a little better," I said as I opened one of the pots on the stove. Rashawn had several pots bubbling on the stove top. It smelled delicious, even though the kitchen looked like a tornado had blown through it.

"Well, you never told me you were working with such a fine man. I would have came by your job, honey," Rashawn said as he pushed me away from the stove.

"That's exactly why I didn't tell you," I said. "I sure don't need your butt down at my job all up in Michael's face."

"Well, at any rate, I'm sorry for actin' a fool at the mall. To make it up to you, I'll allow you to eat some of my good cookin'."

"Oh, I can't. I'm going to Faith Evans's album release party tonight." I turned my nose up at Rashawn as if to say I was better than him.

"Oh really," Rashawn said in a horrible British accent. "I forgot about that. Well, good. That means more food for me and Eli." Rashawn pushed me out of the kitchen. I rolled my eyes at the thought of Eli, but I didn't have time to discuss that with Rashawn. I had a party to get ready for.

The skating rink was crowded with fans. I arrived with Yvette and Michael. The front entrance was roped off, and there was red carpet going from the front door to the sidewalk. News reporters from everywhere, local Atlanta stations and national gossip shows like *Entertainment Tonight* and *Access Hollywood*, were lined up outside the ropes. Just as we were walking into the building, a limo pulled up. Fans immediately began screaming and rushing to the limo. A huge guy dressed in all black stepped out and began pushing people back. Soon after Faith Evans emerged.

She looked fly with her tight hip hugger jeans tucked into a pair of designer boots. As we walked in the skating rink leaving behind the commotion, we could hear the sounds of one of Faith's songs from her first album pumping through the speakers. There were a lot of people in attendance, more than I anticipated. I spotted T-Boz and Chilli from TLC and saw Monica and Jermaine Dupree milling around.

Tammy had done a wonderful job turning the skating rink into a Faith Evans palace. There was a canopy over the skating rink itself and life-size posters of her album cover through out the building. There was a stage in the middle of the rink. Ryan Cameron from V103 was on the microphone announcing the celebrities as they walked in. "Lil Bow Wow is in the building, y'all! We're getting ready to party! Come on, come on!" he screamed into the mic.

Everyone's head turned toward the door as Bow Wow walked in with an entourage of people. I spotted Tammy running around with a clipboard and headset. She looked like she needed help. "Tammy, what do you need me to do?" I asked.

Tammy pointed me toward a table filled with food. "I need you to man the food table until my waiter gets here. He's running late." I grabbed an apron and stood behind the table passing out fancy sandwiches and fruit. The waiter arrived thirty minutes later and relieved me of my duties. The waiter was just in time because Faith was getting ready to perform, and I wanted to be on the front row.

Just as Faith began to sing, I joined Yvette and Michael, who were sipping on drinks along the side of the stage. We listened to her belt out one of her oldies but goodies before she went into her new single. As she sang she looked my way, and we caught each other's eyes; then she winked at me. I thought I was going to pass out.

Faith's new song was very inspirational. She sang about not changing her past if she had to do it all again, learning from her mistakes, and how proud she was of the woman she'd become. The song came from her heart, and it touched mine.

I looked around at my surroundings. A month ago I was in Nebraska involved in a bad relationship struggling to see the surface. Now here I was living in Atlanta. I had good friends, a good job, and a good life. Yvette must have noticed the glow on my face. She turned to me and winked. "Welcome to our family." I was happy.

CHAPTER 4

Tristan

Several weeks went by. I was busy at work trying to prove myself worthy to handle my own accounts. A new pop group called Exodus was having a big event this winter, and they wanted OneStop Events to plan the party. I was eager to get the account. Spending so much time at work, I had hardly seen much of my friends except on Sundays for our usual Sunday brunch.

This particular Sunday it was my turn to host. I really didn't have time to cook, so I picked up a bunch of food from Gladys and Ron's Chicken and Waffles. After church, we all met at the townhouse. I laid out all the food as if I had prepared it myself. Of course Rashawn had to bust me out. "Child, you ain't cook this food!" he said. "This got Gladys written all over it. I can smell it."

"You would have to be the one to say something," I said.

"Well, at least he wasn't cheap," Tyler said as he loaded his plate down with fresh greens and chicken. We all gathered around the table to eat.

"Kim, say grace for us," Rashawn said. We bowed our heads.

"Father God, thank you for the many blessings bestowed upon us. Thank you for the food we are about to receive, and we ask that you forgive us of our sins and save our souls," Kim prayed from her heart. I looked at her and noticed a certain glow. I wasn't the only one to notice.

"Gurl, you meant that prayer, honey. Look at you. Your new beau must be layin' it down right!" Rashawn said as we all started to eat.

"Yeah, honey. I must say you look good, Kim," Tyler added. Eric was too busy eating to notice Kim I guess.

Kim blushed, "He is a sweet man."

"So has he laid the pipe yet," Rashawn blurted out.

Kim's face turned beet red, and that was saying something given her complexion. Even I was embarrassed, but I still wanted to know the answer to that question. Kim leaned in towards us putting her plate of food down on the table. She started to speak in a hushed tone as if she had a deep secret to tell. "Actually," Kim said looking behind her as if checking to see if someone else was listening. "Actually, we finally did it the other day," Kim gushed. It must have been good because Kim was all smiles.

"Gurl, was it good, honey?" Rashawn said.

"Obviously," Tyler chimed in. Rashawn and Tyler gave each other high fives.

Kim smiled. "Yeah, honey, it was good," she nodded her head as if to agree with them. We all fell out laughing.

"So what happened with your little friend from Bulldogs," Eric said interrupting our laughter. I sensed a little sarcasm in Eric's voice. I rolled my eyes at him, and then answered his question.

"He called me a couple of times, but I've been working so hard I haven't had time for him," I replied.

"All I know is all work and no play will leave you dried up all day," Rashawn rebutted. I rolled my eyes again, but thought, *it has been a while since I hooked up with someone*. My hand was getting real lonely.

"I'm sure Eric wouldn't mind satisfying you," Tyler said jokingly.

"Shut up, Miss Thang," Eric shot back.

We ate and talked a little while longer. Rashawn told us about Eli and how he was laying the pipe. Eric bust him out by saying he could have sworn he had seen Eli at a sex party. Rashawn came back with, "What was you doing there, gurl?" We all knew Eli was no good; Rashawn would just have to find out for himself.

As we were wrapping up our meal, my cell phone rang. I looked at the caller ID; it was BJ. We must have talked him up. I answered the phone as I walked outside for privacy.

"Hello."

"Hey, what up wit cha?" came BJ's voice sounding sexy as ever. All that talk about sex had gotten me worked up.

"Hey, BJ. What's up? Sorry, I've been so busy lately," I said.

"Oh, it's cool. Listen what are you doin' tonight? I was thinkin' maybe you could come by my crib," he said.

"Sure," I replied quickly. I didn't know what BJ had in store, but I was anxious to find out. He gave me his address, and I planned to meet him at his apartment at eight.

When I got off the phone I went back into the house. Everyone left shortly after. Kim had to get home to her son; he had gone to church with her mother. Eric said he had to do something at work, and Tyler said he just didn't like spending so much time with a bunch of queens. He was just joking of course.

Rashawn helped me clean up. "So how are you liking it so far?" Rashawn asked as he loaded the dishwasher.

"If you mean my job, I love it," I said.

"So what you sayin, gurl? You don't like livin' with me?"

"No, no, no," I said, "you know I love it here." I thought this was a good time to talk to Rashawn about Eli. "You know, Rashawn," I said hesitantly. I was nervous for some reason. Rashawn could be so unpredictable. "I'm worried about you and Eli," I continued. I looked Rashawn in his face and tried to read his reaction.

Rashawn continued to load the dishwasher. "What are you worried for?" he asked with a confused look on his face.

I stopped wiping the counter and faced him directly. "I mean Eli seems like he's up to no good," I said ready for Rashawn to go off on me.

"Gurl, if you're talking about him being at that sex party, Eric is just jealous and trying to keep up mess." Rashawn had a point there. "When would he have time for sex with someone else when I give it to him on a regular?"

"Okay, Rashawn, I'm just saying be careful." We finished cleaning the kitchen in silence.

~~~

BJ lived in College Park; I had never been to that side of town before; however, BJ gave me precise directions. I pulled into the Winter Green Apartments a few minutes past eight. I looked for apartment C12. There were boys hanging around outside in the parking lot. Some were shirtless; others had their pants hanging below their butts. Young girls stood around trying to catch their attention. It felt as if I was a long way from Tenth and Piedmont.

I found building C, got out my car, and locked my doors. When I knocked on the door, my stomach was full of nerves. BJ answered the door with a bright smile. "Come in," he said in his smooth deep voice. I walked into his apartment. He had the lights dimmed, but from what I could see, he truly lived as a bachelor. There was a couch in one corner and a small television against the wall. There were no paintings or pictures hanging, just a plain white wall. The living room opened up to a small dining and kitchen area. There was no dining table, and the kitchen looked equally as bare.

BJ must have noticed me looking around. "Oh, I just moved in here. Haven't had a chance to do much." I nodded my head. "Would you like a drink?" he offered.

"Water is fine," I said looking him up and down. Boy, did he look good in the sweatpants and tank top he wore. His manhood moved around in his pants like it had a mind of its own. BJ brought me a glass of water, and we sat down on the couch. He sat so close I could smell his Burberry cologne, the same from that night at the club. It was intoxicating.

I looked him in the eyes knowing what we were about to do. "I normally don't do this so soon," I said knowing exactly what we were both thinking.

"Me neither," he responded as he began kissing me on my neck. He felt so good that I just sighed and went with it. Before long, I was following him into the bedroom. We tore each other's clothes off. BJ stood before me naked and beautiful. His arms were enormous. His piece equally so. I pulled him close to me putting my arms around him and squeezing tight. His body was rock solid.

We kissed each other all over, exploring every aspect of each other's body. I left no crevice untouched. Before long he was pulling a condom out of the night table. He laid me down on his bed and parted my legs. I was nervous and excited all at the same time. He proceeded to place the condom on his manhood with ease, and then he gently slid inside of me. It hurt at first. I hadn't done this in a while. Jonathan was the last person I had slept with. But as we got into a groove, I began to relax and feel pleasure.

Our sweaty bodies bounced against each other in a rhythmic time. BJ's moans got louder and louder and my sighs got deeper and deeper. Just when I thought I was going to explode, he pulled out and tore the condom off. He released on my stomach; I came simultaneously. BJ collapsed on the bed beside me. We lay there in the midst of our sex. My body was limp and relaxed. I definitely needed that. Soon, I was in a deep sleep.

~~~

As the weeks went by, the summer got hotter and so did my relationship with BJ. Most of the time we had sex, great sex I might add. But from time to time we went out for dinner or a movie, always out in Marietta or Dunwoody though. BJ said he didn't like going to the movies in his neighborhood. They were too ghetto, and I tended to agree with him, so I didn't mind.

Work was also going well. I was assigned the Exodus account and was meeting them today for the first time. Michael said he would help me out. I got to the office at eight that morning; I needed to prepare my presentation for the group. According to the profile I'd received, they were similar to the Black Eyed Peas. They were a new singing group that consisted of two boys and a girl. One of the boys rapped while the girl and other boy sang.

They wanted to throw a party this winter. It wasn't an album release because their album was already out. I had listened to their CD, and it was pretty good. The group was based out of New York, but they wanted to throw a party in Atlanta to reach a new demographic. The album sales were mediocre, but they were a great group, so their record label was trying their best to promote sales, and it was my job to throw the best party possible.

The group arrived a little after ten that morning. They had flown into town to open for Usher's tour, so I didn't have long to meet with them. Michael joined me in the conference room where they were waiting. Christy was the lead singer. She was tall and thin. She wore long extensions in her hair, and her shorts were so short I thought she was going to get a yeast infection. Efrim was the rapper. He had a nappy Afro and was on the thick side; he wasn't fat, but he wasn't in shape either. However, he was attractive. Monty was the other singer. Now Monty was gorgeous. He had caramel colored skin, thick, wavy hair, and arms that bulged through his T-shirt showing his nice tone.

"Hello, everyone," I said shaking each of their hands. "I'm Tristan, and this is my colleague Michael." I caught Christy and Monty giving Michael the eye and wondered what that was about. They all said hi, almost in unison. I took a seat at the round table where everyone was sitting. Michael joined us.

My nerves were trying to get the best of me. The sun beat in from the window down on my face creating a mist of sweat across my forehead. I wiped my forehead with the back of my hand before I began to speak. All eyes were on me, so I needed to say something to break the ice. "I must say I really did enjoy your album, guys," I said with sincerity.

"Really," Christy said with a smile. She gave you the look of a diva, but really she had a bubbly personality. Her cheerful attitude lightened the mood for everyone, and I relaxed. "Well, I hope you can throw us a fly party," Christy said.

"Yeah, kid, we need to be dope," Efrim added. "We're trying to show Atlanta how we do it," he continued. Monty didn't say much. He just sat back and listened.

I talked to them about the different venues available: Level 3, Visions, or the Compound, the three most popular Atlanta clubs that were large enough to hold a celebrity party of this scale. "Yo, ain't Visions where Diddy be having his Atlanta parties?" Efrim asked.

"Yeah," I replied.

"Well, we ain't trying to copy, man. We're gonna have to do this somewhere else."

I then showed them pictures of Level 3 on Peachtree, and it seemed to be the favorite of the group. They liked the idea of shutting that part of Peachtree down because of their party. We talked about themes and colors and the guest list. By the end of the meeting, I had them all excited. I was even getting excited about all the plans. When the group left to get ready for the concert that night, they all had smiles on their faces, even Monty.

"You did great, man," Michael said after they left. He patted me on the back. Michael and I were still sitting in the conference room going over all the information from the meeting. I had a stack of notes. There was a lot of work to do to pull off such a huge event. I was excited to get started.

"You think I did well?" I asked smiling, knowing I had.

"Yeah, man, good work. Listen, I'm going to work out after work today. You should join me." Wow! Michael was asking me to do something with him outside of work. I was supposed to meet up with BJ later that night, but BJ would have to wait. I wasn't passing up an opportunity to hang with Michael.

Kim

Kim was on cloud nine. She had been spending a lot of time with Brandon. They went on dates several times a week. He sometimes spent the night at her house although she still had yet to see his home. He said he had roommates that were slobs. She was okay with that excuse. Kim even introduced Brandon to Jamal. Brandon seemed like a natural with kids. At times when they were together, Brandon would need to leave all of a sudden. His pager would go off, and he would leave quickly with little reason other than he had to work. He was an electrician and was on call a lot. Kim couldn't be mad at a hardworking man.

Kevin on the other hand was being a pest. He sweated her all the time about Brandon, and today was no different. It was August, and the sun was beaming down. It was ninety degrees by nine o'clock that the morning. It also happened to be Jamal's birthday.

Kim was giving Jamal a little birthday party at her parent's house. She thought about inviting Brandon, but decided against it considering Kevin was going to be there. However, she did invite her Sunday Brunch Club. Rashawn, Eric, Tyler, and Tristan all arrived together, each carrying a nicely wrapped present for Jamal. Kim knew they would go all out.

There were kids running all around the backyard. Kim's mother was in the kitchen mixing up punch, and her father was out back grilling hot dogs and burgers. Jamal was in the midst of all the kids having the time of his life. Presents were piled high on a table under the willow tree where the other parents hung out sipping punch and gossiping.

"Boys, you made it," Kim said as the gang walked up. Kim looked flawless. Her hair was freshly flat ironed, and she wore a sundress and rhinestone sandals. Her legs were smooth as butter, and she smelled like heaven.

"You know we had to come turn the party out, honey," Rashawn said handing Kim his present. Kim collected all the gifts and placed them with the others.

"So where's the birthday boy?" Tristan asked while looking around. As if on cue, Jamal came running up out of breath.

"Hi, Tristan! Today's my birthday. I'm six!" Jamal said holding up six little fingers. He jumped into Tristan's arms.

"I know," Tristan said struggling to hold Jamal up. "You're a big boy now," Tristan said placing him back on the ground.

"Did you bring me a present?" Jamal asked with a sly smile.

"Jamal! That is not polite," Kim said rolling her eyes.

"Child, Tristan ain't the only one standing over here, mister," Rashawn said. We all laughed. Rashawn always had to be the center of attention, even at a child's birthday party.

Tyler escorted Jamal over to where our presents were. "Don't open them yet," Kim said. "We have to wait on Kevin." Kim really didn't want to wait on Kevin, but Jamal meant the world to him, and he was his father.

"Child, this is too many kids," Rashawn said.

"Most of them are kids of my clients," Kim said pointing at the ladies still standing under the willow tree.

"Well, where's the food? I'm hungry," Rashawn said walking toward Kim's father whom was still slaving over the hot grill. Before long, they all sat around eating, laughing, and watching the kids clown around playing games. The party seemed to be going without a hitch, and then Kevin arrived.

Kevin pulled up in his Chevy Impala blasting his music. The bass line was so loud, it shook the house. Kevin got out the car and pulled his present out the trunk. The present was so big he could barely carry it on his own. It was a motorized Tonka truck that Jamal could ride. Jamal had been asking for one for quite some time. When Jamal saw his father with the large present, he stopped what he was doing and ran to him screaming.

"Daddy, daddy, you came, daddy!"

"Of course I came, boy! You MY son, you hear me. You MY son!" Kevin said forcefully. Kim rolled her eyes. "This is MY son, Kim! Don't you forget it," Kevin repeated as if no one heard him the first time.

"Kevin, are you drunk?" Kim glared at him. "I know you did not come to my momma's house drunk!" she yelled. Kevin was stumbling trying to hold his balance. He was sweating profusely. Everyone stared at him. Luckily, Jamal and the other kids were so involved with the toy truck they didn't notice the scene Kevin was making.

"What are you talking about, Kevin?" Kim said getting angrier by the minute.

"I don't want no other nigga takin' care of my shorty," he said. He was stumbling in his words.

"Kevin, I do not have time for this. You need to leave." Kim was almost in tears as her father came running out the back door.

"What is going on here?" he asked in a deep fatherly tone. Kim's tears started to stream down her face uncontrollably.

"I'm leavin'. I'm leavin'," Kevin said. He knew not to mess with Kim's dad. They had been down that road before. "Jamal, yo daddy loves you, man. You 'member dat, man. I love you!" he said as he walked around the front to his car.

"I love you too, daddy," Jamal said barely looking up from his new ride. He hadn't noticed a thing.

The party ended with no further incidents. Kevin sped off leaving Kim there to wipe up her tears. Jamal opened the rest of his birthday presents, and the kids enjoyed cake and ice cream. As the sun set, everyone left. Tristan was the only one who stayed around to help clean up. The night air was cool and a pleasant breeze blew as they began to pack up Kim's car.

"So, are you all right, Kim?" Tristan asked as he cleaned off a picnic table.

"Yeah, I just wish Kevin would get it together. I mean I know he loves Jamal, and I even believe he loves me, but he has to get it together. I can't have my son around all that drama." Kim had cleaned her face up; you would never have known she had been crying.

"Well, he seems to be upset that you are dating," Tristan said. "By the way, how's that going?" he asked as they began loading the car.

"It's good," she said. "I just wish we could spend a little more time together. He's always working and having to leave all the time. How are things going with your friend? What's his name again, EJ or BJ, something?" Kim asked.

Tristan smiled thinking about all the good sex he was having. "His name is BJ, and it's good. Unfortunately, I keep thinking about Michael. You know we work out together now?" Tristan said.

"I didn't know that," Kim looked shocked. "Tristan, you better be careful. I don't want your feelings getting hurt. If he's straight, don't be catching feelings for him knowing nothing could ever happen." Kim was genuinely worried for Tristan. "Do you think he's gay?"

"Honestly, Kim, I don't think he is. I think he just likes being my friend. I mean he helps me out at work a lot, and when we work out, we talk about everything you could imagine. I think he just likes having a good friend."

They packed up Kim's car and even loaded up Tristan's car. Tristan was going to follow Kim to her house and help her get settled in. He kept looking at his watch for the time. He didn't want to miss going to BJ's house for his weekly fix.

By the time they pulled up in front of Kim's house, Jamal was knocked out sleep. Tristan carried him into the house and laid him on his bed. He helped Kim unload the presents and food. As they were unloading, Kim's cell phone rang. She looked at the caller ID. It was Kevin's sister. She was in no mood to deal her either. She was just as ghetto as Kevin, and besides, Kevin was probably having her call for him. Kim pressed the silent button on her phone. She was tired and just wanted to go to bed. Once everything was unpacked and Kim was settled, Tristan took off.

Between all the children at the party and dealing with Kevin, Kim was exhausted, so she readied herself for bed. As she was putting on her night clothes, she picked up her phone to call Brandon. She noticed she had twenty missed calls, all from Kevin's sister. Why was she calling back to back like that? Kim began to worry. She dialed Kevin's sister's number. The phone rang several times before someone answered.

"Where the fuck have you been?" Kevin's sister Tawanda was screaming in Kim's ear. She sounded as if she were crying.

"Tawanda, calm down! What's wrong? What do you want?" Kim said dreading the worst. Kim began pacing back and forth in her bedroom waiting for Tawanda to say what was going on.

"It's Kevin, bitch. He's been in a car accident. He's down here at Grady in critical condition. We been calling yo ass for hours!"

Kim's heart sank. She didn't know what to do. She dropped the phone on the floor. She could hear Tawanda screaming through the phone. Kim's body began to tremble. Her heart pounded so hard it felt like it was going to burst out her chest. Everything suddenly began to move in slow motion. Kim opened her mouth but nothing came out. She wanted to scream at the top of her lungs, but she didn't want to wake Jamal. Kim quickly dialed her mother. She would know what to do.

As Kim's mother picked up, the tears started to flow. It must have been the soothing sound of her mother's voice, or it could've been the guilt of knowing she'd sent Kevin into the streets drunk. Kim's mother came over right away to sit with Jamal while Kim rushed to the hospital. Kim was afraid of the worst; she loved Kevin for the simple fact that he was her son's father. If anything happened to him, Jamal would be devastated. She cried for Jamal, she cried for Kevin, and she cried for herself all the way to the hospital.

CHAPTER 5

Tristan

Time had flown by since I'd arrived in Atlanta. It was already August. I had just gotten home from Jamal's birthday party, and I was exhausted but determined to meet up with BJ that night. As I was headed home to change, I looked at my phone to check the time and noticed I had a couple of voicemails. One was from Michael telling me he was not going to be able to work out this weekend. We had started working out three times a week, twice during the week and once on the weekend, usually Saturday. We were actually becoming good friends. I trusted him with my inner secrets. It was like having a straight best friend, something I was not used to. The other message was from BJ. He had called to tell me I couldn't come by. Something came up, and he would hook up with me another time.

Damn, I thought to myself, *I could use some of BJ's good loving.* I guess there was nothing left to do but go home. As I pulled up to the townhouse, I noticed Eli sitting on the front stoop. I rolled my eyes. Rashawn must not have been home yet. I parked the car and walked up to the front door, pretending like I didn't even see Eli sitting there.

"Yo, kid, I been waitin' out here fo an hour! Where dat Rashawn at?"

"I don't know," I said as I unlocked the door. Eli got up from his seat. I could feel him standing behind me breathing down my neck. *Where the hell was Rashawn*, I thought.

"You gonna let me in, right?" Eli asked.

I opened the door, and we went in. I barely said anything else to Eli. He made me feel so uncomfortable. He walked around like he owned the place, and he always looked at me as if he wanted to jump my bones. Once we were in the house, I immediately went upstairs to my room and shut the door behind me. I left Eli downstairs to do whatever until Rashawn got home. It had been such a long day, and I needed to take a shower. I went into my bathroom and turned the water on hot.

The steam poured from the shower leaving a mist on the mirror as I took my clothes off. I stayed in the shower for as long as possible. The water felt good on my body. I was very tense, and the pellets hitting my body relaxed me. I was looking forward to my bed. I wrapped a towel around my waist and opened my bathroom door to let the steam escape. "What the HELL!" I screamed.

What I saw shocked me into reality. Eli was standing in my room completely naked. His piece was hard as a rock not to mention as long as his arm and leg put together! He looked sexy as hell, but wait a minute. "Eli, what are you doing?" I asked standing there in shock. I put my arms over my chest as I realized, besides the towel around my waist, I was naked also.

"Yo, kid, you mean to tell me you don't want this?" Eli motioned toward his manhood which stood at perfect attention. "You know I been checking you out, kid. You be walkin' round here wit dat fat ass. You know you want me to tap dat," he said.

Oh my goodness! I couldn't believe this was happening to me. It was as if I had stepped outside of my body, and I was watching this scene play out in slow motion. Before I could say another word, I heard a loud scream. Standing right behind Eli was Rashawn. He just appeared out of nowhere.

"What the fuck is going on in here?!?!" Rashawn yelled at the top of his lungs. He looked like a mad man. His hands were on his hips, and his face was beet red.

"Yo, shorty," Eli started, but he wasn't able to get two words in before Rashawn started swinging on him. Eli's only defense was holding his hands in the air.

"I'm gonna fuck both you bitches up! Y'all up here having sex!" Rashawn had lost his mind; he actually thought Eli and I were having sex. I quickly grabbed a pair of jogging pants that were thrown on my bed. I was not about to fight without clothes on.

"I can't believe this shit!" Rashawn screamed as he continued to punch Eli. "I knew something was going on between you two. I knew it!" Just when I thought Rashawn was coming for me, Tyler appeared out of nowhere.

"Rashawn, calm down!" Tyler screamed as he grabbed him from behind. Eli managed to get away from Rashawn long enough to run downstairs and out the door. Rashawn tried to run at me, but Tyler had a strong grasp on him.

"Get out my house, bitch! I caught you red-handed! Get out!" Rashawn was ranting and raving. Foam started to form around the corners of his mouth.

I couldn't believe this was happening. Rashawn really believed something was going on between Eli and me. I was utterly stunned; I thought Rashawn was my friend. Tyler was still struggling with Rashawn trying to get him to calm down.

"Baby, I think you better go," Tyler said to me with sympathy in his eyes. Where was I going to go? I didn't have any family in Atlanta? I grabbed a couple of items and threw on a T-shirt. I ran out the front door and hopped in my car, not knowing where I was going.

As I drove I started to cry. How did I get in this mess? I dialed Kim's number but kept getting her voicemail. I didn't want to call Eric, and Tyler was still back at the house trying to get Rashawn under control. I finally dialed Michael's number. He was the only one left that I could trust.

"Hello," Michael answered in a low voice.

"Michael, I'm sorry to disturb you," I said trying not to sound as if I was crying.

"No problem, what's up?" he asked.

I started to tell him the story of events that had just played out. "I really don't have anywhere to go," I said.

"Don't worry, Tristan," Michael said. "You can come over here. I have a spare room. Don't worry about it, man." I sighed with relief. Michael became my personal savior. As Michael gave me directions to his place, I began to feel a little better.

Michael lived in a high-rise not far from Lenox Square Mall. The entrance had a doorman, and I had to be announced before I was allowed to pass the main entrance. I was instructed to take the elevator to the eighth floor. From the looks of it, Michael was making much more money than I was. Michael came to the door wearing a T-shirt and sweatpants. Even dressed down he was gorgeous. "Come on in," he said motioning me into his place.

His apartment was fabulous; the carpet was a thick, plush white, so white I was scared to step on it. The living area had a huge bay window that overlooked the city. A plasma screen hung on one wall, and there was African art on the other wall. Sitting on the couch with a drink in her hand was a beautiful woman. "I'm sorry," I said realizing I was interrupting.

"Oh, it's okay," Michael said. "This is Tracy." She smiled at me.

"Hi, how are you?" she said. Tracy had a warm, inviting smile and a sweet disposition. Although she seemed polite, I felt uncomfortable, like I was interrupting a date or something.

Michael showed me the spare room. It had a fluffy, queen size bed with plenty of pillows. There was a desk in one corner and files stacked up against the wall. The room obviously doubled as his office. Up against one wall was an armoire that housed a television. "Make yourself at home," Michael said leaving me alone to get settled. Once I got my things together, I went into the living room. I wanted to ask Michael where he kept his towels. I found Michael sitting on the sofa flipping through the channels on TV.

"Oh, I'm sorry, Michael. I didn't mean to run your friend off," I said.

"Oh, no. It's cool; she was just leaving when you showed up anyways."

I wanted to ask who she was, but I thought that was really none of my business. I joined him on the couch. Michael grabbed a couple of beers out of the refrigerator, and we sat and watched football. I can't say I knew what was going on. I'd learned to pretend really well from watching my brother play in high school, but I wasn't a football fan. I was just glad to be with a good friend because I was feeling really lonely at that particular moment.

Kim

Kim tried not to speed on the way to the hospital. She didn't want to end up in a bed next to Kevin. Once she got there, she ran into the emergency room waiting area where Kevin's family was. Tawanda, his sister, was pacing the floor; his older brother was there as well as his grandmother and mother. His father was in prison, so he wasn't able to be there. Kevin's mother, Ms. Bristle, ran to Kim and embraced her. She always liked Kim. She was the only one with any sense in their family. Even the grandmother was crazy.

"Kim! I'm glad you came."

"Ms. Bristle, how is he?" Kim asked.

Kevin's mother could barely contain her tears. "He flew through the windshield, bitch! How you think he is?" Tawanda interrupted.

Kim ignored her; she knew she was just upset. Under normal circumstances, Kim would have checked Tawanda. Even now she wasn't going to be too many more of Tawanda's bitches. "Kim, he's in a coma," Ms. Bristle said between tears.

Oh my God, Kim thought. What was she going to do? Every thought imaginable ran through her head, and then the tears started to flow. She didn't want Kevin to die. She wanted him to get his life together. Kim sat with the family in the waiting room, waiting on an update from the doctor. Kim began to get anxious, so she called Brandon. He would be able to console her and make her feel better.

He sounded busy, but when she explained what was going on, he came right over. She needed his support; she needed him to hold her. She didn't want to upset the family, so she met him outside. As soon as he wrapped his arms around her, she broke down.

~~~

Eric had gone into work after Jamal's birthday party. He needed to finish up some work before the weekend. He was trying to get a promotion, so he was going over and beyond the call of duty. Eric enjoyed working at Grady Memorial. It was like a live soap opera everyday. Eric worked in admissions, but floated between the ER and admissions whenever the help was needed.

Today when he came in, it was as busy as ever. He noticed on the roster for new patients a Kevin Bristle. *Is that Kim's Kevin,* he thought as he rushed to the ER department. Just as he rounded the corner, Eric got his answer.

There was Kim standing outside the sliding doors. She seemed to be crying, and she was hugging a man. They were in a deep passionate embrace, so Eric could only assume it was Brandon. She had talked about him so much that Eric pretty much knew what he looked like. As Eric peered around the corner, Brandon lifted his head and Eric froze. They caught each other's eye for a split second then Eric quickly ducked around the corner.

Did he see me? Eric thought Then Eric realized the windows were tinted so you couldn't see in, only out. Thoughts were running through Eric's head. What should he do? For now, nothing. He went back to the admissions area, did the work he came to do, and left without Kim even knowing he was there. As he worked, he said a silent prayer for Kevin.

CHAPTER 6

Tristan

*M*ichael was a gracious host. He went by Rashawn's place to pick up some of my things, and when Kim called and told me Kevin had been in a car accident, Michael offered to go to the hospital with me. He also told me I could stay with him as long as I needed. Of course I was looking for an apartment of my own, but at least I didn't have to rush.

Jamal's birthday turned out to be one of the worst days of the summer. Kevin was in the car accident, I was homeless, and I still couldn't believe Rashawn thought Eli and I were having sex. I mean I know it looked suspicious, me and Eli standing there with no clothes on, but I thought Rashawn knew me better than that. I thought we were friends.

As the week went on Kevin remained in a coma, and we all took turns babysitting Jamal while Kim was at the hospital. She wasn't ready to take Jamal to the hospital just yet. Since everything seemed to be going crazy, I decided to throw myself into my work. Christy,

Efrim, and Monty from the group Exodus were coming into town this week to take a look at Level 3, the club we had decided on. I was able to get V103 involved with the party, and we had several celebrities who confirmed they would be in attendance. My first event was coming together quite nicely.

My friendship with Michael was really starting to blossom as well. If only he was gay, he would be an even better lover.

I went to see Kim a couple of times while she sat with Kevin at the hospital. She tried to talk to me about Rashawn; of course I didn't want to hear it. She said he didn't seem to be doing very well. I figured Rashawn was just being the drama queen that he was.

Kevin finally came out of his coma; however, he was a long way from getting out of the hospital. The car accident had caused a lot of damage. He had been speeding and wrapped his car around a pole; it was a blessing that he was even alive.

Exodus, or as I called them "The Group," came into the city on Friday. I met them at the airport, and we were heading straight to the club. As I stood at the entrance to the terminal waiting for them to come up the escalator, I heard a commotion. I didn't know what was going on and found myself hoping it wasn't a terrorist attack. I guess 9/11 had really done a number on everyone because I was really scared of airports. I looked around to see if others were getting nervous. Then I saw where the commotion was coming from.

Christy, Efrim, and Monty were coming up the escalator, and there was a mob of kids and a few adults crowded around them. Cameras were snapping, and children were screaming. Christy looked like a true diva. She had on huge glasses and carried a large Louis Vuitton bag. Efrim looked grungy as usual, but Monty was in rare form. He wore what was possibly the tightest shirt known to man. It showed every ripple in his stomach, and he seemed to be loving the attention the most, smiling and signing autographs.

Wow, I thought to myself. These were real celebrities that I was working with. As they got off the escalator, I greeted them.

We collected their bags, and before long, we were being whisked downtown in the limo that I had waiting outside.

The limo was the first purchase I'd made with my new company American Express card, and it was well worth it. A big difference from driving around town in my little Neon. The leather seats felt like butter, and there was wine and sodas for everyone to enjoy as soft music played in the background. While in the limo, I went over some details of what I had been working on.

"So, guys, I spoke with your manager, and she thought it would be a good idea if you performed at least one song." I looked at their expressions as I relayed this message. I had already known that they did not want to perform; they just wanted to enjoy the party. However, their manager wanted them on the stage, and I agreed.

"Tristan, I thought this was supposed to be a party, not a concert?" Christy said with a pouty voice.

"Hey, man, I don't feel like singing." That was the most I'd heard from Monty in a long time. Efrim, on the other hand, was all for performing; that's what he lived for, so I didn't get any complaints from him. I debated back and forth with them, but in the end, they knew they really didn't have a choice.

Once we arrived at our destination, we took a tour of the facility and discussed color scheme and design. Before long, we parted ways. They were scheduled to appear on a couple of radio shows that day, and I needed to get back to work. As I was saying my goodbyes to the gang, my cell phone rang.

"Hello," I said not checking the caller ID.

"Hey, what up, boy?" It was BJ, and his voice sounded good to me. I hadn't spent time with him lately. I pictured him talking to me naked. Man, I was lusting for him.

"Hey, what are you doing?" I said already getting aroused.

"Nothing, man. I haven't seen you, and I was just wondering if you wanted to grab a bite to eat with me today." Of course I did. We made plans to get together for dinner that night at The Cheesecake Factory in Buckhead.

That invite made my day. I went back to the office and rushed through the rest of my day, cutting out early to get a jump start on my date. I walked out to my car excited about my evening with BJ. We usually didn't go out. Most of the time we stayed in and had amazing sex. Him taking me out was a sign to me that he was interested in going further in our relationship.

It was a beautiful, early evening. The temperature was just right for a date. I walked out to my car and noticed a piece of paper on my windshield. It looked like a note. *God, I hope someone hasn't hit my car and left a note.* I grabbed the paper and read it quickly. In nicely typed print, the note read:

> *Be careful of whom you deal with.*
> *It just might blow up in your face.*

What the hell, I thought to myself. This must be Rashawn playing a dumb game with me. I didn't have time to deal with his mess. I crumpled the note up and tossed it on the ground. I watched the wind blow the crumbled piece of paper down the street. As I hopped in my car, I cleared my thoughts of Rashawn. I needed to get home and change for my date with BJ. I opted to wear a pair of blue slacks and a V-neck tee. The slacks were a little snug in the butt area, but that was okay. I wanted BJ to get a good look at what was in store for him later.

I met BJ in front of the Cheesecake Factory at eight. The restaurant was packed to capacity. BJ was standing out front of the building looking as sexy as ever. He wore a brown, knit shirt and tan slacks. His muscles bulged out of every inch of his shirt.

When he spotted me, he gave me a huge smile that made me feel like I was the only one on the face of the planet. "Hey, boy. How are you doing?" he asked in that deep, velvet voice. I shivered. I wanted

G. L. Johnson

to jump his bones right there in front of the restaurant. His scent was so intoxicating that I thought I was going to pass out.

"Hey," I said all smiles with a few butterflies in my stomach. I don't know if it was nerves or if I was just a little hungry. We made our way through the bustling crowd. Luckily, BJ had arrived early, so we were able to be seated right away.

Our waiter was a pimple-faced teenager. He sat us at a booth toward the middle of the restaurant. As we took our seats, he placed menus in front of us and asked for our drink orders. The restaurant was very noisy, so I had to practically yell to be heard. I ordered a Mandarin Sour. I had no idea what it was, but it sounded good. BJ ordered a Bud Light. How boring.

As the waiter rushed off to get our drinks, I looked across the table at BJ. His lips were so luscious and sweet. I felt an urge to lean over and kiss him, but I held in my urge. We were in a public restaurant, and although Atlanta was pretty liberal when it came to the gay lifestyle, the city wasn't that liberal. I mean I didn't want to get stoned right there in the middle of the restaurant. BJ smiled back at me with that sly smile he gave when he was trying to be coy.

"What're you thinking 'bout, Tristan?" BJ asked as he looked over his menu.

"I was just thinking how happy I was that you invited me on a date," I said lying. I was actually thinking let's skip dinner and go straight to dessert. We talked for a few more moments before our waiter hurried back with our drinks and took our order. I decided to have the chicken salad; I wanted to eat light because I didn't know what the evening might bring. After we placed our orders, BJ abruptly excused himself from the table to go to the restroom, leaving me there alone.

I looked around the restaurant. Many couples were there. People were eating, talking, and laughing, and some were even cuddled next to each other kissing. I spotted a beautiful, black woman walking towards my table. Wait a minute, it was Kim!

She walked up to me with a huge smile. Once she reached my table, I stood up to give her a hug. "Kim, what are you doing here?" I said as we embraced. Even after all she was going through, she still looked good. Her face had a look of worry, and you could see sadness in her eyes, but she was still as beautiful as ever.

"My girlfriends decided to take me out for dinner to get me away from the hospital for a bit," she said pointing towards a pack of girls standing at the front door. There were four girls, each one was just as glamorous as Kim.

"Well, are you coming or going?" I asked.

"Oh, we've already eaten. We were leaving, and I saw you sitting over here alone," she said.

"I'm not alone," I replied with a smile. "I'm here with BJ. He went to the restroom. You can meet him if you'd like." I was excited about Kim meeting BJ. I talked so much about him, it was time she put a face with the name. Just then one of Kim's friends walked up.

"Kim, I'm sorry, but we've got to go. I promised I'd pick up my son by nine." I recognized Kim's friend from Jamal's birthday party.

Kim turned to me, "Oh, Tristan, I'm sorry. I'd love to meet BJ, but I have to go. Call me later. Love you, boo." With that she was gone. I smiled to myself. It was good to see Kim out and in good spirits; Kevin's accident had really taken a toll on her. I made a mental note to remember to buy her a card to show how much I cared.

Before long the food came. It was piping hot and smelled delicious. BJ had ordered a steak, and I was tempted to cut a piece. I was so caught up in the aroma of the food, and a little buzzed from the liquor, that I didn't even notice that BJ was still not back from the restroom. In fact, I didn't notice until the waiter said something to me about it. I looked around and hoped he was okay. I was getting ready to get up and go look for him when he came walking up to the table. He must have noticed the disturbed look on my face because he apologized immediately.

"I'm sorry, baby," he said. "I got a phone call that I had to take." He flashed me his million dollar smile, and with that everything was right with the world. I didn't give it another thought. The food was great, and the conversation was even better. Before long, we were back at his place in the midst of a night of passion. I must have put it on him something fierce because he was out like a log.

As BJ snored, I watched him sleep. He looked like a little boy sleeping peacefully with a smile on his face. As I lay next to him, I looked up at the ceiling and daydreamed about what it would be like to have BJ as a permanent boyfriend. He seemed to always have something going on, but all in all, he seemed to be a good guy, and the sex was the bomb. As I lay there and thought of my future with BJ, I began to doze off. Before long I was awakened by the sound of BJ's pager vibrating across the nightstand. I looked over at BJ who was still fast asleep; the night sky cast a shadow across his face and made him look like an angel. His soft snores were labored and deep. I reached over him and grabbed his pager. I don't know what made me do it, but when I looked at the pager and saw 911 flashing after the phone number. I called the number back, making sure I dialed *67 to make my number private. The phone rang only once before a woman's voice answered.

"Hello!" said an angry voice from the other end. I froze I didn't know what to say. I wasn't expecting a woman to answer, and I wasn't expecting her to sound so angry. "Hello! I know you hear me! Say something damn it! Where the fuck are you?" she yelled.

Obviously she thought she was talking to the person she'd paged. I listened to her voice trying to make out who it was, but of course I couldn't.

"Well, fuck you then," she said just before I heard the dial tone as she slammed the phone down in my ear.

What was that about? Maybe it was a wrong number or maybe it was someone BJ knew. At any rate, something didn't feel right. I eased over BJ and placed his pager back on the nightstand. I was trying to be as still as possible so that I wouldn't wake him. BJ moved slightly as I reached over him. His chest heaved up and down as he breathed deep. Just as I placed the pager down I felt something grab my arm. My heart started to pound in my chest. *I'm busted,* I thought; now I'm going to have to find a way out of this mess.

"You ready for round two, baby?" BJ said as he grabbed my arm and pulled me on top of him. That was a close call. BJ began rubbing my body as he got aroused, and soon we were enthralled in a second helping of good loving. As BJ did his thing, I lay there, my mind wondering. How well did I know this man? What secrets did he have hidden? Did he have a crazy baby momma? Or worse was he married? I didn't know what to think, but I knew I needed to get to the bottom of it.

Chapter 7

Work was becoming increasingly hectic. It was the end of August, and the Atlanta heat was in full force. I was still living with Michael, and I was working hard trying to get this project off the ground at work. I hadn't seen much of BJ since the last time I spent the night a couple of weeks ago when I almost got caught checking his pager. I was a little uncomfortable with him. There was something I didn't trust about him.

This particular day I was headed into the office early. Usually Michael and I would ride together, but I needed to get some work done so I headed out around eight leaving Michael still fast asleep in his room. It was already eighty degrees, so I knew the day was going to be a scorcher. My forehead immediately formed sweat pellets when I stepped outside. I turned my air conditioner on full blast when I got in my car and listened to Frank and Wanda in the Morning on V103. Frank and Wanda were in the middle of talking about deadbeat daddies and child support when my cell phone rang. It was my mother.

"Hey, ma," I said with a smile on my face.

"Good morning, baby. I have good news," my mother said in a gleeful voice.

"What is it?" I asked looking forward to some good news in my life.

"You have a new little nephew; Corey Jr., born this morning around five," she announced proudly. I was ecstatic; I had forgotten that Corey had a baby on the way. I was so caught up in my own life that it had slipped my mind.

"Oh, ma, wow! Corey must be so proud. I'm going to have to make a trip home to see the baby," I said feeling warm and tingly all over. I knew Corey was happy; he always wanted a little boy. His first born was a girl. Diamond was a beautiful little girl, and Corey loved her dearly, but secretly he dreamed of having a son. I knew this because he confided in me a couple of times about how he wanted a son to carry on the family name. "Mom, that is great. Tell Corey I'm so happy for him."

"Tell him yourself. He's right here with me," she said before handing Corey the phone.

"Yo, man, I got a son, Trey." Corey and Kim were the only two people who called me Trey.

"I know man," I said. "I'm happy for you. Who does he look like?"

"Man, you know he looks like his pops. He looks just like me." I could practically see the beam on Corey's face through the phone. At that moment I wished I was back in Nebraska. I missed my brother. We didn't get a chance to talk often, but I wished I was there to share that special moment with my family. "When are you coming back for a visit, Trey? We miss yo butt here in the big O," he said taking the words right out of my mouth.

"I don't know, Corey, but I'm going to try to make it home really soon. Listen, give Nisi my best and let her know I said congratulations. Make sure you treat her right, Corey," I said being the big brother.

"Aight, man, I love you. See you soon, big bro," he said before hanging up. What a way to start the day. I had a new nephew. I immediately called 1800Flowers and ordered two dozen roses to be delivered to Nisi and Corey in the hospital to show my love. I knew Nisi would love them. I reached the office at around 8:30 a.m., just as I was finishing the order for the flowers.

"Good morning, Yolanda," I said with a bright smile as I walked in the office. Yolanda was not a morning person, and you could tell. She usually didn't speak to anyone until after ten.

"What are you so chipper about?" she asked with her usual morning attitude.

I smiled, "My brother just had a baby boy. I have a nephew now."

Even grumpy old Yolanda couldn't hold back her smile. "Oh, that's nice, Tristan! Congratulations!" she said handing me a few messages and some mail.

"I'm so happy for my brother," I said as I walked into the office. It was quiet in the office. Most people didn't come in until around 9:30 a.m. As I walked to my cubicle, I noticed Yvette's light on in her office. I peeked my head in. "Good morning, Yvette," I said.

She looked up from her computer. Obviously, she was deep in thought. "Hey, Tristan. How's it going? You working hard?" she asked. On top of the big Exodus project, I also helped with other smaller events.

"I'm doing okay. Trying to get this Exodus party going," I said.

"Well, I hear you've been doing very well, Tristan. You seem to be holding up to your word," she said referring to our interview when I was first hired. She looked back at her computer as if to let me know she needed to get back to work. Yvette was a cut to the chase, no nonsense kind of person. She didn't spend much time with small talk. I took that as my cue and headed to my desk.

I looked over my messages. The promoter for Level 3 called; also I had a message from Exodus's band manager. I made a note to call both of them later. I had an envelope that was unmarked with no return address. There wasn't even a postage stamp on the envelope. Just my name printed neatly on the outside of the envelope. Someone must have hand delivered the note. I tore into the envelope and pulled out the one slip of paper inside. The note was typed and read:

You have been warned.
Take heed of your surroundings.
And be careful of your friends.

The note was very similar to the other one I had received. I immediately went to the front desk where I found Yolanda filing her nails. "Hey, Yolanda, who delivered this letter? There's no return address," I said showing her the envelope.

"Tristan, I don't know. It was stuck to the door when I came in this morning." Yolanda rolled her eyes and went back to filing her nails.

Okay, I thought to myself, *if Rashawn wanted to play games, I could play right along with him.* I went back to my desk and called Tyler on the phone.

"Hey, Tristan. What's up? Long time no talk to," Tyler said when he answered the phone. I hadn't really seen much of Tyler or Eric since I moved out of Rashawn's place. So much had happened. We weren't even having Sunday brunches anymore.

"Good morning, Tyler," I said. I cut straight to the chase. "Listen, could you tell Rashawn to leave me the hell alone? I'm trying to put that ugly incident behind me, but he is really testing me." I was getting angrier as I spoke.

"Child, what did he do now? You know Rashawn can be a mess sometimes," Tyler replied.

I explained to Tyler about the two notes I had received. "Tyler, he is coming to my job now. I ain't got time for drama at my job!" I said.

"Well, I'll call him today and see what's going on," Tyler replied.

"No! Call him now!" I said ready to get to the bottom of this mess. Tyler kind of hesitated. I could tell he didn't want to get in the middle of my drama, but I needed this to stop immediately. Tyler put me on hold and clicked over and dialed Rashawn's number. After what seemed like a million rings, Rashawn finally picked up.

"Hello," Rashawn said in a groggy voice. It was weird to hear his voice after all these weeks of not talking to him.

"Hey, Rashawn," Tyler said sounding a little nervous. I just sat on the other end silent. I wanted to hear what Rashawn had to say. I sat in my cubicle and slouched down real low so no background noise could be heard. "Were you sleeping, Rashawn?" Tyler said.

"What you think, gurl," Rashawn shot back. That was odd because Rashawn was usually up at the crack of dawn. Rashawn always had an early client. He felt that time was money, at least that was what he was always saying to me.

"Oh, I'm sorry to wake you, Rashawn," Tyler continued, "but I was calling about Tristan." Rashawn let out a loud sigh. "I know you don't want to hear about him, but he's been receiving threatening letters . . ."

Rashawn cut Tyler off. "I know you're not suggesting I'm sending that little sissy threatening letters? Come on, Tyler. You know me better than that," Rashawn said with disgust. "You tell Tristan . . . No how 'bout I tell Tristan cause I know he's on the phone . . . Tristan, stop being a whore and then maybe you can sleep better at night! You must be sleeping with someone else's man 'cause it ain't me sending you threatening letters."

My eyes got wide and my mouth fell open, but not a sound came out. Rashawn slammed the phone down leaving Tyler and me on the line.

"Tristan? Are you all right . . . hello," Tyler said.

"I'm here," I said feeling dumb. "Well, baby, I'm sorry about that, but I really don't think Rashawn is the kind of person to send little notes. You be careful out there because it sounds like someone is out to get you." After that Tyler said goodbye because he had to go to work.

I sat there still holding the phone in my hand thinking. Rashawn had said something that hit hard . . . "You must be sleeping with someone else's man." Those words rang loud and clear. I pondered my situation the rest of the day. I didn't have a clue who could have been sending those notes. I called Kim; she would know what to do.

"Hey, Tristan," she said sounding extra chipper when she answered the phone.

"What up, Kim? How are you doing?"

"I'm good, Trey. Just at the shop doing a little hair. You know trying to make that money," she sounded in much better spirits.

"You sound like you are in a good mood," I said.

"Well, I feel a little better. Kevin's doctor said he's going to make it. He has a lot of broken bones, but there was no brain damage from the coma. In fact, Kevin is already talking, laughing, and getting on my nerves. Of course, I'm just so glad he is alive," she said.

"You love him don't you?" Kim was silent and that gave me my answer. "Kim, I think I need to talk to you," I said interrupting the silence. She could tell I was upset by the sound of my voice.

"What's wrong, Trey?" Kim responded sounding concerned.

"Can I come by?" I really wanted to talk to Kim in person.

"Sure," Kim said, "I'll be at the shop all day."

"Okay, I'll be right over," I said. I took an early lunch and headed to Kim's beauty shop.

Kim's shop was located in downtown Decatur and was owned by an older woman named Ms. Rita. Ms. Rita was in her sixties. She wore big wigs and too much makeup. She had been the owner of Ms. Rita's Hair Salon for nearly forty years, and it was well past time for her to retire. Kim should've been the owner; she drew in the most clientele. Men came in to get haircuts just so they could look at her, and women loved how Kim made each of them look like celebrities by the time they got out of her chair. Kim was good at what she did.

I parked my car in the parking lot on the side of the building and went inside looking like a diva myself with my large sunglasses, slacks, and tie. I had on a pair of new Ferragamo shoes that made a clacking sound on the granite floor. When I entered the shop, all eyes turned to me. That was one thing I hated about going to black hair salons. It was like going to a fashion show because if you weren't dressed right you would get talked about, and even if you were dressed nicely, you still got talked about. Luckily, I looked nice.

Ms. Rita greeted me from behind the front desk where she always sat. She claimed she was a hairstylist; however, I never saw her with any clients. I think she liked sitting up front so she could be nosey. The shop was set up with four barbers in the front and six hairstylists in the back. The stylists were Kim, Lisa, Bonita, Latoya, Cassandra, and Walter. Of course Walter had to be a flaming queen. The few times I'd met him, he hit on me loud and outright, and today was no different.

Walter was at a washbowl washing some overweight woman's hair. He was older, probably in his early forties. In his younger days, he was probably a good catch because he wasn't bad looking now; however, you could tell the streets had worn heavily on him.

"Oh, Miss Tristan, don't you look diva-ish. Come, baby, and give me some suga," he said to me. The male barbers all looked our way, probably to see what I was going to do.

I blushed. "Hey, Walter," I said. "Where's Kim?" I continued, totally ignoring his request.

"Oh, she's in the back," he said motioning his head toward the back of the shop. "Miss Thing, you gone have to be still before you get soap in your eyes, and then you'll be crying," Walter said to the pleasantly plump woman sitting at the washbowl.

Kim walked in from the back storage, and of course she looked great. She had a black smock draped over her, but you could still make out her slamming figure. "Hey, Trey," she said with that bright smile.

"Hey, Kim," I said as we embraced.

"You smell good," Kim said taking a double sniff of my neck. "That scent is so familiar to me. By the way, thank you for that lovely card. Your words of encouragement meant a lot to me," she said giving me another hug.

"Dang, girl, how come I don't get hugs like that?" one of the barbers asked.

"Shut up, Kenny," Kim said laughing. "Let's go outside, Trey. These folks are going to be all in our business." We went outside and sat on the benches in front of the shop. Kim's next client wasn't due in for another hour so we had time to talk.

"How's Jamal doing?" I asked.

"Oh, he's good. I finally took him to the hospital to see Kevin. Of course he had a million and one questions, but he's handling it well. It's good now that Kevin is awake and can talk. He's just in a lot of pain."

I rubbed Kim's back in an affectionate way. I swear if I was straight I would love to date Kim. A couple of cars passed by and honked at Kim as we sat outside in the heat. Kim was very popular.

"So what's on your mind, Trey? I know you didn't come down here to talk about Kevin and Jamal."

"You're right, Kim. I didn't," I said as I started to explain the letters I had received. I also told her about BJ's pager and what had happened when I called the number back.

"So what did the woman say, Tristan?" Kim said as she listened intently to the story. She had a way of making you feel like she truly cared about you, and I believed that she did. That was what I liked most about Kim.

"Well, Kim, she didn't say much. She just kept tying to get me to say something, like she knew who I was on the other end," I said.

"Well, baby, you need to be careful. I mean I don't know this BJ, and it could be a coincidence, but you can never be too sure. You need to pray about it. We all need to pray. It's been a while since we've all been to church together. Let's go this Sunday," Kim said as she reached over and gave me a hug.

"Who do you mean by all of us?" I asked thinking about how much I didn't want to see Rashawn; however I knew she was going to include him.

"I mean all of us, Tristan. You and Rashawn are going to have to see each other eventually," Kim said sounding more like my mother than my friend.

"Well, I guess church is as good a place as any to run into Rashawn," I replied. So we made plans to go to church that Sunday. Kim said she would call Rashawn, Tyler, and Eric, and she wasn't going to take no for an answer from any of them. I already knew she was going to have a hard time convincing Rashawn.

CHAPTER 8

*S*unday came way too fast. I spent the rest of the week working hard on getting the setting designed for Exodus's party. The group had decided on a winter wonderland theme with plenty bling bling, or as they called it ice. We were going to call the party "Winter's Paradise." They wanted to do it big with ice sculptures and diamonds everywhere, so that kept me busy for the rest of the week. I talked Michael into coming to church with me. I needed that extra support if I was going to have to deal with Rashawn. Of course Michael was okay with joining me for church. He had a church he belonged to, but he was up for a visit to another church.

I woke up Sunday morning with butterflies in my stomach. I was nervous about seeing Rashawn. Kim said she had the hardest time trying to get Rashawn to agree to come to church. She didn't think he was doing to well. I was way too nervous and needed to calm down, so I got on my knees and prayed. I asked God to give me strength to deal with Rashawn and to give me a forgiving heart. I felt better after I prayed, so I jumped in the shower and got dressed.

I met Michael in the living room; he was already dressed sitting on the couch watching a football game waiting on me. "Man, you take forever to get dressed," Michael said.

I smiled. "When you look this good, it takes time," I said, even though he had me beat in the looks department. Michael wore a three piece suit that looked so good on him that it should have been illegal. The deep royal blue of his suit went well with his dark black skin.

"Well, Brother Tristan, let's go get our praise on," Michael said. We took Michael's car to the church. Michael had a Lexus Coupe; it was black with beige leather interior. It felt good riding in a luxury car. The ride was smooth and peaceful. We listened to Praise 94.1 FM, the local gospel station.

We arrived at the church around 10:45 a.m. We were a little early for the eleven o'clock service, but it was already packed. I spotted Kim and Tyler in a pew close to the front of the church. "Hey, Kim," I said giving her a hug. "You remember Michael."

"Hey, Michael. God bless," Kim said smiling as she gave Michael a hug.

"Same to you, Kim. It's good to see you." Michael shot back his Colgate smile.

Tyler cleared his throat as if to be noticed. "Oh, Michael, this is my friend Tyler." They shook hands, and Tyler looked at me and gave a wink. I laughed to myself. I was sure I was going to hear from Tyler about Michael.

Eric came in a few moments later. "Good to see you all," he said as he took a seat next to me. He was breathing heavy like he had just finished running. "I had to run in here before Rashawn did," he said. We all looked at him confused. Eric continued, "Rashawn was walking up to the church at the same time I was, and, honey, I was not prepared for what I saw."

"Where is he now?" Kim asked.

"He's in the restroom, and, baby, let me tell you he don't look good." *Eric's a drama queen,* I thought. *He must be exaggerating.* Just as I finished my thought, I was proven wrong. Rashawn walked in, and as if on cue the choir stood up and started to belt out a song to start the service. I looked directly at Rashawn. Our eyes met for just a few seconds before he looked away. This time Eric wasn't exaggerating. Rashawn looked horrible.

He had cut his dreads off, but he didn't have a fresh hair cut. It was kind of choppy and nappy and actually bald in certain areas. He had facial hair, which Rashawn usually never let grow out, and he looked like he had lost about twenty pounds, which was saying something since he only weighed around 130 pounds initially.

He walked over to where we sat moving at a very slow pace. He spoke to everyone except me; he even spoke to Michael. Everyone pretended like everything was okay, but we all had the same look on our face. We all knew something wasn't right.

Rashawn took a seat at the end of the pew next to Kim. I noticed Kim grab Rashawn's hand and rub it as the choir sang. A tear formed in the corner of my eye. That was why I loved Kim; she was so caring. I wanted to run to Rashawn and give him a hug, but my pride kept me in my seat.

The choir sang several songs constantly making the church jump to their feet. Michael seemed to really enjoy himself, rocking to the music and shouting out praises to the Lord. There was nothing like a man who wasn't afraid to show his religion. The Bishop came out shortly after and began delivering a sermon about God's love. He said God loved us all, no matter what we had done in our lives. God was almighty, and He had already forgiven us of our sins. Bishop Morton told us to turn to our neighbor, say "God is almighty," and give them a hug.

Michael and I embraced as we repeated what the pastor said. His embrace was tight and strong. It sent sparks off inside my body. I couldn't tell if it was the Holy Ghost or the attraction I had towards

Michael. I looked at Michael in the eyes and mouthed the words "God Bless you" and he did the same. I looked down at Kim and Rashawn who were embracing. I noticed a few tears in Rashawn's eyes, but I looked away quickly.

As I sat listening to the Bishop preach, I noticed a woman sitting a few rows up. She kept looking back at me. She looked like a young woman in her early thirties perhaps. She was okay looking, her hair was pulled back into a bun; she was brown-skinned with worry lines around her eyes. I noticed her because every time we made eye contact, she would look away. I couldn't remember ever seeing her in church before, although she looked familiar, like someone I might know.

Before service was over, Rashawn said he had to leave, so he couldn't have brunch with us. Kim protested, but he left anyway. When church was over, I made my way to the strange woman that had been staring at me. She was headed out at a fast pace, but I grabbed her arm just as she made it to the front door.

"Ma'am, excuse me," I said. "Do I know you from somewhere?"

She turned towards me, but never looked up. "I don't think so," she mumbled.

"Are you sure? I mean I noticed you staring at me during service." People had started making their way to the vestibule, and it got a little noisy. Old church ladies were standing around talking about where they were going to eat while little kids ran around happy to be out of church.

"Sir, you don't know me. Now if you would excuse me, I have to go," the strange lady yanked her arm out of my hand and dashed out the church. I could've sworn that I knew her, but I must have been mistaken.

I joined the gang outside the church where they were waiting on me. "Who was that woman you were talking to?" Kim asked.

"I don't really know what that was," I said looking puzzled. "She was staring at me in church like she knew me."

"She probably just thought you were cute, honey," Tyler said.

"Yeah, that's it," I agreed as we all got a laugh at my expense.

We decided to eat at a place called Cow Tippers; the restaurant was located in Midtown Atlanta, not far from Piedmont Park. It was a nice summer day; the temperature was cool enough to be able to sit outside while we ate. As we were seated, I noticed Tyler had taken a few extra peeks at Michael. I leaned over and whispered in his ear, "He's straight, girl. Leave that alone." Tyler laughed.

"Hey, no secrets," Michael said.

"They're probably talking about you," Eric replied. Our waiter came to take our orders just in time. I was a little hungry, so I decided to have steak and a martini.

"Oh, that sounds good," Tyler said. "I think I'll have the same thing." Michael ordered a Caesar salad, and Kim had a chicken sandwich. Eric decided to have the steak as well.

"Y'all boys sholl do love your meat," Kim said laughing. We were enjoying a nice brunch until Eric changed the subject.

"So what was up with Rashawn?" Everyone got quite all of a sudden. "I mean I know y'all saw how bad he looked," Eric continued.

"When did he cut his hair?" Tyler added. The mood of the table switched from laughter and enjoyment to gloom.

"Well, I know this makes you feel good, Tristan," Eric said.

I shot Eric an evil stare. "Eric, I'm not that kind of person. I don't wish any ill will on Rashawn. I'm not like you!" Eric looked at me with surprise in his eyes like he couldn't believe I had just said that.

"Girl, pick up your lip," Tyler said to Eric. "We all know you're a snake in the grass." That lightened the moment up, and we all laughed.

"I just pray he's all right," Kim said. "I think I'm going to go by his house after I leave here," she said sounding concerned.

"If you guys are that worried, you should all band together as friends and stand by him," Michael said while giving me a little push. I guess that comment was meant for me, but how could I stand by Rashawn when he couldn't even stand by me. At any rate Rashawn needed help in every sense of the word.

CHAPTER 9

Kim

Kim was extremely worried about Rashawn. After seeing him in church, she knew something was terribly wrong. Kim had already gotten information that Rashawn wasn't doing well, but she hadn't shared it with her friends. Kevin's friend, Reggie, had told her several months ago that Rashawn had purchased some marijuana from him. Kim dismissed it as him buying it for one of his boyfriends, but then Reggie said that Rashawn had upgraded to coke, and lately he was buying on a regular basis. Kim knew that Rashawn and Eli had broken up, so he could only be buying the drugs for himself, and after seeing how bad Rashawn looked, she knew it was true.

Kim's heart was heavy for Rashawn. They had met when he came into her shop to get his dreads done by one of the stylists who focused on natural hair. Kim loved him immediately. He was loud and obnoxious but full of joy. He was always making her laugh and always told her the truth. He stuck by her when Jamal had gotten sick, and he always lent a shoulder to cry on when Kevin was acting up. Rashawn was a dear friend; now it was Kim's turn to be a good friend.

After the brunch everyone said goodbye, and Kim headed straight to Rashawn's house. Hopefully, he would be home; he'd cut out of church in such a hurry, she wasn't sure where he'd gone.

Kim pulled up to the front of Rashawn's townhouse. Everything looked normal from the outside; however, she knew looks could be deceiving. There didn't appear to be any lights on and all the curtains were closed. She thought about calling first, but she knew he wouldn't answer the phone.

Kim knocked on the door. The pit of her stomach began to turn. She was scared as to what was happening on the other side of the door. She knocked again, yet no one came to the door. "Rashawn!" Kim yelled out . . . still no answer. Kim reached in her purse and pulled out the spare key Rashawn had given her. She recalled when he had given it to her.

"Gurl, now don't be just coming in my house unannounced. I might have some trade boy in my bed, honey," he'd proclaimed with laughter. Kim was to only use the key in case of an emergency. This was as much an emergency as any she could think of. She turned the lock and slowly opened the door.

"Rashawn? Hello? Are you in here . . . honey, it's Kim," she said. The living room was dark, but she could tell everything was still in its place. If his house was any indication on how he was doing, then it looked like everything was normal. Kim began to walk up the stairs. Each step she took made her feet feel heavier and heavier. Once she reached the top of the stairs, she could see directly into Rashawn's room.

"Rashawn, sweetie, it's Kim . . . you okay?" she called out in a meek voice. No response came back. Kim went further, making her way into Rashawn's bedroom. Amongst all the blankets and pillows, Kim could make out a tiny, frail body. On the night table next to the bed were several large pill bottles, all of which were opened. Kim ran to Rashawn screaming. "Rashawn! Oh my God! Wake up! Rashawn!" She shook his body praying to God he wasn't dead. As she shook him, tears started to run down her face. The room was dark and had a strange scent to it. "Oh, God, Rashawn!" Kim screamed franticly.

"Gurl, if you don't stop shakin' me. I ain't no rag doll," came the weak voice from under the pillows.

Kim took a deep breath. "Oh thank God!" Rashawn lifted himself up from under the covers. Kim gave him a once over to make sure he was okay. "You scared me, Rashawn," Kim said giving him a tight squeeze.

"Why, child?" Rashawn replied. Kim motioned towards the medicine on the night stand. "I know you didn't think I had killed myself. Honey, you know Miss Thang can't go out like that?" Rashawn winked at Kim.

"Rashawn, I'm serious. What's going on? You are not the same Rashawn that I know" Kim was struggling to find the right words to express to Rashawn. She knew she had to be delicate with her choice of words. She wasn't trying to piss Rashawn off. "I . . . I . . . I know about you buying the drugs Rashawn." Kim stammered, "Be real with me."

Rashawn got a serious look on his face. His mood immediately changed. Kim knew whatever he was about to say that it wasn't going to be good. "Kim, I'm sick," Rashawn said in a solemn voice.

"Oh no, Rashawn! You have AIDS? I'm so sorry," Kim reached over to hug him.

Rashawn abruptly pushed her away. "See, that's why I didn't tell anyone. NO, Kim! I don't have AIDS or HIV!" Rashawn glared at Kim. "Just 'cause I'm gay and sick, doesn't mean I have AIDS. I mean I know I like to have sex, but I'm not stupid."

"Well, then what is it, Rashawn?" Kim asked wanting Rashawn to get to the point.

"Kim . . . I . . . have . . ." Rashawn's voice kind of drifted off for a moment as if struggling to get the words out. "I have cancer, Kim," he finally said.

Kim's mouth fell open in disbelief. Rashawn had always looked so healthy. "Rashawn, how long have you known this?"

"Now, girl, I'm going to have to swear you to secrecy," Rashawn said. Kim crossed her heart with her fingers. Rashawn went into how he had cancer before he moved to Atlanta but had been in remission for over a year. "Kim, I really thought all of that was behind me," he said with tears in his eyes.

"When did you find out it had come back?" Kim asked.

"Right before Tristan moved in," he replied. Rashawn explained that he had acute myelogenous leukemia, which was a severe form of cancer. "Kim, I just didn't want to deal with it," Rashawn continued. He talked about how Eli was a good distraction for him, but Eli liked to do coke, and not here and there. He liked to do a lot of coke. "I began doing the coke with him, and it felt good, Kim." Rashawn had a far away look on his face. "The drugs allowed me to escape from what I was dealing with," Rashawn said.

"Drugs are not the answer," Kim said with compassion.

"I know that now, Kim," Rashawn said frowning at her. "Drugs are not for me. I was going downhill too quickly, and if I'm going to go out, I'm going to go out in style," he said.

"Rashawn, don't say that. You can make it. You can beat this," Kim said sounding hopeful.

Rashawn explained how his only hope was a bone marrow transplant and that was highly unlikely to happen. "That's why I agreed to come to church, Kim. I was getting lost out here by myself." Rashawn broke down at that point. He cried into Kim's arms, and Kim cried with him. She knew although Rashawn had a tough exterior he was a soft little boy on the inside. She knew he needed someone to love him. Luckily, she knew how to love.

They sat in the darkness of Rashawn's room for what seemed like an eternity, but was in actuality only a few hours.

"Okay, gurl, enough crying. I got it out my system," Rashawn proclaimed as he threw the covers back and climbed out of bed.

"We need a game plan," Kim said.

"What do you mean a game plan? This ain't football, honey?" Rashawn said looking confused.

"No, Rashawn, I mean we need a game plan for getting you back on track, and I'm here to help," Kim proclaimed as she jumped up. Kim had a surge of energy and a head full of ideas. She ran to the curtains and drew them back, exposing light into the room that had been missing it for weeks. "First thing, we have to do something about that hair, Rashawn."

Rashawn looked at himself in the floor length mirror in the corner of his room. He frowned with disgust as if it was his first time seeing himself. His hair had fallen out from the chemotherapy treatments he was receiving. One night after an intense chemo treatment, he came home and chopped his dreads off leaving behind the nappy patchwork that he now wore.

Kim walked up to him and ran her hands through his hair. "We can give you a fade. I'll have one of the boys from my shop do it." Rashawn smiled. He hadn't felt this hopeful in a while.

"Okay, girl, I guess," Rashawn said trying to hide his glee. It felt good to him to have someone willing to be by his side.

"Then after that we are going to get you and Tristan back to being friends."

"Oh no, Kim! That ship has sailed," Rashawn said changing his attitude.

"Rashawn, you know he did not sleep with Eli. He is your friend." Rashawn knew this was true. Several days after the incident happened, Eli confessed that he and Tristan didn't do anything. Eli was just a sex-crazed whore. However, Rashawn had his pride. How could he admit to Tristan that he was wrong?

"Just leave that alone," Rashawn said. Kim agreed, but only for now. She was eventually going to get the two of them back together. She just knew it. Kim and Rashawn finished their game plan discussion, and Kim agreed to go to the doctor with Rashawn for moral support.

Kim headed out shortly after they finished. She felt good and optimistic about Rashawn. On the other hand, as Rashawn watched Kim walk to her car, he knew the truth. There wasn't much time left. He waved goodbye from the front door wondering how many more goodbyes he had left.

CHAPTER 10

Tristan

"Mom, I feel so bad. What am I supposed to do?" It was Wednesday, and I was at work talking to my mother. Kim had relayed the news to me about Rashawn, and now I was relaying that news to my mother.

"Honey, all you can do is pray. Pray for Rashawn and leave it in God's hands." My mother spoke so eloquently as if she had all the answers in the world.

"I just wish we could put that ugly situation behind us," I said feeling sorry for Rashawn.

"In due time, Tristan, in due time. You have to give Rashawn time; that's all." I knew what my mother was saying was true. It was just going to be hard not being able to be there for Rashawn like I wanted to be, but I guess not everything was about me. "Well, Tristan, I have to go. Corey's coming by with the baby, and I need to get this house in order. Remember to pray, baby."

I hung up the phone. As I did, my phone immediately rang. "Hello," I said.

"Tristan, you have a call," Yolanda said.

"Oh, ummm, who is it?" I asked a little confused since everyone who knew me called my direct number.

"They didn't say, but I'll transfer it to you now," Yolanda said. A few seconds later a muffled voice came across the line.

"Is this Tristan Smith?" the distorted voice said.

"Yeah, who is this?"

"That doesn't matter," the stranger replied. "You need to watch your back before you end up dead!" the voice said before slamming the phone down.

I sat there holding the phone in my hands trembling. I was in disbelief, who could be out to get me? I didn't even know many people in Atlanta. The caller said I needed to watch my back; obviously, someone was trying to hurt me, but why? I must have been sitting in the same position for a while because Michael walked up to my cubicle with a look of worry on his face.

"Hey, Tristan . . . what's wrong? You look like you've just seen a ghost." I told him what had just happened. "Man, you have too much drama going on in your life," Michael said.

I rolled my eyes. "Tell me something I don't know."

"Come on, man. Come with me."

"What, Michael? I have work to do," I protested.

"So what. You need a break."

"Where are we going?"

"Just trust me," Michael replied. That was just it. I didn't know who to trust.

We were soon in Michael's car driving through downtown Atlanta. For a midday work week, there sure was an awful lot of traffic. Why weren't these people at work? I sat in the passenger seat oblivious to where Michael was taking me. He whipped through the city streets like a seasoned pro. He maneuvered his Lexus in and out of traffic leaving everyone in his dust. He commanded the road just like he commanded everything else in his life.

I snuck a few peeks at him as he drove. His eyes were fixed intently on the road, his attention totally on his destination. I pushed the power button on his CD player. "Do you mind if I play some music?"

"Sure, if you don't mind listening to my kind of music," Michael said. Nina Simone came through the speakers. Her eclectic voice mixed with smooth jazz rhythms flooded my ears. It certainly wasn't what I was used to hearing, but it was nice. "You like Nina Simone?" Michael said.

"Well, I don't know. I never really listened to her," I said being honest.

"She's the bomb, Tristan," Michael said. We listened to the music as he drove through the city. Before long we were pulling up to a large house in a not so great neighborhood. There was a small playground in front of the two-story, Victorian style house, which was encased by a metal fence. Michael parked in front of the house.

"Come on. Don't look so scared," Michael said as he got out the car. I followed behind. There was a sign out front that read "Heaven's House"; it looked like some kind of childcare facility. As I followed Michael through the front door, I became a little nervous about what I was going to find.

In the foyer of the house was a reception area where a young woman sat flipping through a magazine. "Hey, Michael," she said with a bright smile.

"Hey, Tosha. How are you?" Michael responded. "This is my friend, Tristan." Tosha was an intern from Clark Atlanta University. Soon as we were done with introductions, the door behind Tosha opened up.

"Hey, Tracy," Michael said. It was Tracy, the girl from Michael's house the day I moved in.

"Mike, hey, hon," she said walking up to Michael and giving him a hug. She was flawless. Her hair was pulled back into a neat bun, and she had on a tailored suit that showed off her womanly curves. Any man would fall over backwards for her. "I see you brought company," she said turning to me.

"You remember Tristan," Michael said.

Tracy extended her hand for me to shake. "Of course I remember," Tracy said with a warm smile. She had the kind of smile that was infectious.

"Nice to see you again," I said.

"You ready, Mike?" Tracy said. I was still so confused.

"What are you ready for, Michael?" I asked totally out of the loop.

Michael laughed. "I'm sorry. Tracy is the coordinator here at Heaven's House. I come and read to the kids twice a month, and sometimes I play games and mentor."

"What is Heaven's House?" I asked still confused.

"Well," Tracy stepped in, "we are like a foster home for kids with terminal illnesses. Many of our kids have HIV, cancer, some are handicapped. Most of them will die sooner than later, and most do not have parents." Tracy went on to say how the program is totally funded by donations, grants, and volunteers like Michael.

I followed Tracy and Michel into a room that looked like the living area. There were several large sofas and a television in one corner. Kids were already seated waiting for Michael to begin his story. When Michael entered the room, they all cheered and shouted out his name. "Mikey, Mikey! Hi, Mikey!" they said with joy in their eyes.

There were about twelve kids waiting to be read to. Tracy stood in the back with me as we watched Michael take center stage. As Michael engaged with the kids, Tracy educated me on Heaven's House.

Heaven's House was founded by a woman named Patricia Gibson. Patricia's daughter was diagnosed with cancer and died at age nine, ten years ago. Patricia wanted to do something to make a difference, so she started this home, which was named after her daughter, Heaven. The kids ranged in age from newborn to eighteen. The oldest in the house now was fourteen. Tracy said most of the children didn't make it out alive, succumbing to their illness. However, some did get adopted.

Heaven's House was a place the kids could call home. Tracy and Michael went to college together and were great friends, so when Tracy took the job as coordinator of the facility, Michael began volunteering. Obviously, he enjoyed spending time with the kids; as he read aloud to them, his face glowed. He was in rare form. Tracy said every year they have a big fundraiser in January, and OneStop Events coordinated the event for free. "Michael has really been a blessing," Tracy said with a twinkle in her eye. It seemed as if Tracy had more than just friendship feelings for Michael.

As Michael finished reading to the kids, I looked around at the children. Most of them were African American. There was one little white boy and one Asian girl, but the rest were black. All of them looked relatively health. From an outsider looking in, it looked like a group of kids at your local elementary school. The kids milled around Michael asking questions and tugging on his leg. One little girl caught my attention.

"Hi, mister," she said looking up at me, her eyes big and round. She was so beautiful; I kneeled down to talk to her on her level.

"Hello there," I said feeling a little nervous. "What's your name?"

She smiled, flashing her pearly white teeth. "Alicia," she said as she put her hand over her mouth to cover her smile.

"My name is Tristan. Nice to meet you, Alicia. How old are you?"

She held up six fingers.

"Six," I said. "Oh, wow, you are a big girl!" I proclaimed.

"Would you like to play with me?" she said grabbing my hand pulling me towards the little toy area in the corner of the room. I followed. Alicia set up a pretend tea party with all the fixings. Her imagination was enormous. "You can be the prince, and I will be the princess at our tea party," she announced. I played with Alicia, and she laughed and giggled the whole time. We had a whole tea party celebration together complete with stuffed animals who were our servants.

Before long Michael was tapping me on my shoulder. "Tristan, we have to go," he said pulling me back into reality. I had gotten lost in Alicia and our world of make-believe.

"I'm sorry, Alicia. I have to go, but I'll come back to visit," I promised her, and I meant it.

"Wow," I said as Tracy escorted us to the front door. "Why is she here?"

"Her mother died of AIDS last year, and she also has full blown AIDS. She has no other family that is willing to take care of her. She was shuffled from foster home to foster home until she ended up here," Tracy explained.

My heart broke. That precious little girl with no one to love her. As we turned to leave, I heard the sound of a little voice calling my name. "Tristan, Tristan!" I turned around. It was Alicia running toward me.

"What's wrong, Alicia?" She ran to me and threw her little arms around my legs.

"I forgot to give you a hug goodbye," she said. I bent down and picked her up. I gave little Alicia the biggest, tightest hug I could give. Her tiny arms wrapped around my neck. I smiled a bright smile as I placed Alicia back on the ground. She waved goodbye from the doorway as we headed back to the car.

That was just what I needed to put my life back into perspective. "I can't believe you volunteer there," I said to Michael once we were in the car headed back to work.

"Why not?" Michael replied.

"Not in a bad way. It's just what don't you do? It seems like you have life all figured out, like you don't have any problems," I said to him sounding a little envious.

"Well, I wouldn't say that, Tristan. I have my share of problems." I looked at him trying to see if he had any hidden secrets that could be revealed in his eyes. "Tristan, you have to find a balance in your life and learn to deal with the things you cannot change."

"I'm trying, Michael. But it's hard."

"It's not hard, Tristan. You are just making it hard," he replied. Michael pulled his car into his reserved parking spot at the office. We got out the car and headed into the office. "Eliminate those people in your life who are bringing you down," Michael said as we went into the office.

CHAPTER 11

I thought a lot about eliminating unnecessary people, and I knew what I had to do. I needed to cut my ties with BJ. It would hurt like hell, not because I was in love, but because I was really going to miss the great sexual encounters we had. I mean the brother knew how to lay the pipe.

Although I didn't know for sure if my problems were at all connected to BJ, my intuition was telling me something wasn't right. So it was settled. I would call him that night when I got home and break it off. I left work around six that evening, a little late since I had to tie up some loose ends for the Exodus event. I was exhausted having had such a long day. It seemed like days ago when I had visited Heaven's House with Michael when in actuality it was only hours ago. I hopped in my Neon and popped in my Jill Scott CD.

Jill Scott was another one of my favorite artists. Although completely different from Beyonce, she ranked right next to her with me. The diva had a voice that wouldn't quit. I sang along to her live version of "Long Walk" as I drove through the hectic rush hour traffic. I tried to come up with different ways to tell BJ I didn't want to see him anymore. I even considered just not answering his phone calls, but that was the cowardly way out.

I pulled up to Michael's high-rise. I was going to miss living here. I had really gotten used to the life of luxury over the short time I'd been staying there. The night doorman greeted me as I walked up. "Hi, Rudolph," I said giving him a wave.

"Good evening, Mr. Smith," he replied as he opened the door for me.

Once inside the apartment I made myself comfortable. I needed to relax, so I threw on my favorite flannel pajama bottoms with my "I'm spoiled" T-shirt and turned my television to Lifetime to catch a couple reruns of *The Golden Girls*. Michael had an event to be at, so I knew he wouldn't be home until late. I had the big fancy apartment all to myself. Once I was comfortable, I picked up the phone and dialed BJ's pager number. He called right back.

"Hey, sexy. What up with you?" he said sounding seductive.

"Hey, BJ," I tried to be stoic and to the point.

"What's crackin', man? I haven't heard from you. I've been missing you, man."

I wasn't going to allow him to seduce me; I was calling for a reason. *Stay focused, Tristan. Stay focused.*

"BJ, we need to talk," I said trying my best to be serious.

"What's up, man?" God, that voice drove me wild.

"BJ, I don't think I can see you anymore." There. I'd said it. Now it was out in the open.

"What?" BJ shouted over the phone.

"I'm sorry, BJ, but there is a lot going on in my life. A lot has happened that I haven't even told you, and I just feel like I need to be alone to focus on me right now." Phew, I got all that out in one sentence.

"No, I don't think so, Tristan," BJ said sounding very assertive. I don't know what I was expecting BJ to say, but that was certainly not it.

"What?" I replied a little stunned. I muted my television and sat up straight in my bed. I know this man didn't just tell me no.

"Man, Tristan, I'm having a good time with you, and I know you're having a good time with me. Why do we have to stop? What did I do to you?" BJ pleaded.

I really didn't feel like going through this with BJ. I just wanted to end it and be done with it. "Where are you at now?" BJ asked.

"Um, I'm at home. Why?"

"Because if you're gonna break it off with me, I want you to say it to my face."

Oh no! I can't let him come over here.

"BJ, I don't think that . . ." He cut me off

"Where do you live? I can be there in twenty minutes," he said.

What was I doing? I was supposed to be dumping him, but before I knew it I was giving BJ directions to the apartment. Call me weak-minded, but I caved in. I was determined to be done with BJ after his visit. I changed into a pair of baggy jeans and a sweatshirt. I didn't want to call any attention to my body. I wanted to look as unattractive as possible. Shortly after I changed my clothes, the house phone rang. I already knew who it was before I answered it.

"Hi, Rudolph."

"You have a visitor, Mr. Smith. It's a gentleman by the name of BJ," Rudolph said in his proper doorman tone.

"Send him up," I said and before long BJ was knocking on the door. I waited a few moments before answering; I wanted BJ to think I was busy. After a couple of knocks, I finally opened the door. BJ stood there in the doorway looking as sexy as ever. He must have been working because he had on a pair of dirty work boots, some tattered jeans, and a T-shirt, yet he was still ravishing.

"This yo spot, man? You living nice," BJ proclaimed as he attempted to walk in. I stopped him in his spot.

"Take them dirty shoes off," I said. He obliged, and I let him in.

"Man, this crib is tight," he reiterated.

"It's not mine. I'm staying with a friend"

"Well, I like your friend's taste," he said as he gave himself a tour. I followed close behind him as he made his way through the kitchen and into the living room. "What a brother got to do to be living like this?"

"Work hard," I replied being short with him. BJ turned around to face me grabbing my waist and pulling me close.

"What's this about you don't want to see me anymore?" His sweet scent drifted up my nostrils.

"BJ, let me go," I said struggling to get out of his grasp. BJ held on tight. He looked me dead in the eyes. It felt like his stare was going to burn a hole in my head. "BJ stop!" Then his tongue was in my mouth. Before I could get another word out, we were engulfed in a deep passionate kiss. He tasted so sweet. His tongue rolling around in my mouth with ease, as if swimming through an ocean. He reached down and grabbed my butt, squeezing it tight and making me moan gently.

"Now tell me you don't want me," he whispered between our kisses. I wanted to tell him I didn't want him. I wanted to say I didn't trust him, and my life was in danger. But I couldn't. My knees were weak, and my brain was mush. All I could think about was the hard tool he had between his legs. I led him to my bedroom, and he threw me on the bed. We wrestled and tugged at our clothes till we were both completely naked. I guess there was nothing wrong with one more round of love making before I let him go.

~~~

My body was like jello. BJ had worked me over well into the night. The loving was so good that we were both in a deep coma until early that next morning. As BJ lay next to me I was awakened by the sound of Michael's voice calling my name from outside of my door. "Tristan, wake up! Turn on your television . . . wake up, man!"

I heard him say as I opened my eyes trying to adjust to the light. I looked over at BJ who was still sound asleep. What was Michael yelling for? Just as I was sitting up, Michael burst through the door. "Tristan, turn your television to channel three! Tristan . . ."

Michael stopped in his tracks when he noticed I wasn't alone. "Oh, I'm sorry, man. Ummm . . . ummm," he stumbled over his words. My eyes were as wide as a deer caught in headlights. Michael looked away. "I didn't mean to interrupt, but you need to turn on your TV to Atlanta Alive news," he said as he quickly exited my room and shut the door.

I was so embarrassed. Michael and I had never discussed anything about me having company. I felt like I should run to him and explain. As I pulled the covers back, I realized I was still naked. Guess I'd have to talk to him later. I grabbed my remote from the nightstand and turned my television to the news. BJ still lay comatose snoring beside me. The anchor man was delivering a breaking news story.

"Singer Monty Wilson of the group Exodus was arrested this morning on charges of lewd conduct in Los Angeles. Monty was allegedly soliciting sexual acts in a local park outside a Los Angeles suburb from an undercover male police officer." My mouth dropped opened. *Did he just say MALE police officer?*

The reporter continued to say Monty was released early this morning on a $50,000 bond and was expected in court in September for an arraignment. Wow! Monty was soliciting sex from a male cop. This meant that Monty was gay, or at the very least bisexual. I couldn't believe it. I immediately jumped out of bed and looked at my clock. It was 7:20 a.m. I quickly showered and dressed. I needed to get to the office. When I was done getting dressed I grabbed my keys from the nightstand. That's when I noticed BJ still sound asleep in my bed. I had completely forgotten about him.

"BJ, get up! You have to go," I said as I shook him out of his sleep. My cell phone had already begun to ring off the hook.

BJ moaned and groaned. "What time is it?"

"Time for you to go," I replied trying to sound urgent. BJ got out of bed, his manhood at full attention. I wanted to service him once more, but I didn't have time. I helped BJ get his clothes on and rushed him to the front door, saying goodbye for the last time. Michael was coming out of his room fully dressed for work as I shoved BJ out the front door. I turned to Michael as I shut the door.

"Hey, Michael, we riding to work together?"

Michael hadn't looked at me in the eyes yet. With his head hung down he replied, "Um, well, Tristan, I have something I need to do today, so we better take separate cars." There was an awkwardness in the air, and I knew he was avoiding me because of the scene in my bedroom.

"Okay, well, I guess I'll see you at work," I said as I headed out the door. I had work to do. I already had messages from several sponsors threatening to pull out of the Exodus event. V103 left a message saying they needed a statement from Monty or they would pull out. When I got to the office, Yvette was there waiting on me.

"Looks like we have a scandal," Yvette said with a smile.

"What are you smiling for?" I asked rushing to my cubicle. She followed behind me.

"Scandal is good, Tristan. The more publicity, the more interested people are going to be in our event."

"But, Yvette, this is bad publicity."

"You know the saying," she replied, "any publicity is good publicity. In our case, you just have a lot of work to do."

"Well, I guess I better get started," I replied. Yvette left me to my work. I sat there for a few moments to collect my thoughts and plan my next move. I knew something was different about Monty. I recalled our first meeting when he didn't say much, but he kept staring at Michael. I recalled the obsession he had with his body and appearance. I just equated it to him being a high maintenance celebrity, but he was really a stereotypical gay man.

I got Monty's manager on the phone. Richard Giles was the manager for the group. I had never seen him before, but I'd had several conversations with him over the phone. He was a fast talker, and you always felt like he was pulling a fast one on you.

"Tristan, my main man," he said quickly when he answered the phone.

"Hey, Richard."

"Look, I know why you're calling, but we are still green lit for the December party," he said.

"Well, Richard," I said trying to get a word in.

"Tristan, don't worry. We are working on getting a press release now. I just bailed Monty out of jail, so we have to get focused but give me a few hours," he went on, not listening to me at all.

"Richard!" I said, "I need to . . ."

He cut me off. "I'll call you later today." With that he hung up. Richard could be so difficult.

I dialed Monty's number, but it went straight to voicemail. I really needed to get in touch with Monty. My brain was working in overdrive. I thought for a moment then picked up the phone and dialed another number.

"Hello Tristan," came the angelic voice of Christy, Monty's bandmate.

"Hey, Christy! How are you?"

"Oh, wonderful, I'm sure you heard the news," she said. It was odd she sounded strangely cheerful considering this could affect her career.

"Yeah, Christy, I heard this morning. You seem to be in awful good spirits about all this," I said.

"Well, of course I am. I've been trying to get Monty to come out the closet for years, and now he has no choice."

"So you knew he was gay?" I was stunned.

"Of course I knew. Monty is my cousin. We grew up together, and I've known since we were young, but he insisted on remaining in the closet," Christy explained.

"Well, Christy, I need him to give me a call ASAP. He needs to give a statement to V103, or they are threatening to pull out of the party," I said sounding a little exasperated. Christy assured me she would have him call me. I checked my watch. It was fifteen minutes to nine. There was an hour and fifteen minutes before the Frank and Wanda Morning Show ended. Hopefully, I could get Monty patched in before then. Christy and I chatted for a few more minutes, then we said goodbye.

I made a few more calls to sponsors trying to smooth things over. My final call was to Tiffany & Co. They were sponsoring the jewelry that would be worn by Monty, Efrim, and Christy the night of the party. They were also going to have a display that accompanied the ice theme. Luckily, I was able to talk them into staying involved. As I hung up with the rep from Tiffany & Co., my phone immediately rang.

"Hello, this is Tristan," I said trying to sound professional.

"Honey, I knew that man was gay!" It was Tyler.

"Tyler, what do you want?"

"I was calling to get the dirt, honey. Eric and Kim are on the phone too, child."

"Hey, Trey," Kim announced.

"Good morning, guys," I said.

"What's up, Tristan?" Eric said still trying to sound like some thug boy. I never understood why he couldn't just be himself.

"So, child, spill the dirt," Tyler said eager to get me to start talking.

"Well, guys, I don't know very much more than you do. I got the information from the news just like you did," I admitted. I didn't tell them what Christy had confided in me. It wasn't my place.

"Awww, that's no fun," Tyler said jokingly.

"Well, Tristan, that's not the only reason we called you," Kim said.

"It isn't?" Tyler said laughing.

"Be serious, Tyler," Kim said.

These guys are a mess, I thought. "What's up, Kim?"

"Well, you all know the news about Rashawn and his cancer by now," Kim announced. We all let out low groans. It was difficult to think about Rashawn being that sick.

"Yeah, I know," I said.

"Well, you know he needs a bone marrow transplant," Kim continued. I knew where she was going. Kim went on to explain how she thought it would be a good idea if we all went and got tested to see if we were a match for Rashawn.

"Kim, do you think he'll want my bone marrow?" I asked.

"He doesn't have a choice if he wants to live," Tyler answered for Kim.

It was settled. We all agreed to be tested. "Maybe you can talk Michael into getting tested. I mean the more the better," Kim said.

I sighed. I had forgotten all about the scene that morning with BJ and Michael. Kim made me remember.

"What's wrong, Tristan?" Kim said sensing my distress.

"I think Michael is upset with me," I admitted. I explained how Michael walked in the room while BJ and I were in bed together.

"Why do you think he's upset?" Tyler asked. "Do you think he wanted to be the one in bed with you?" he said.

"No, no," I quickly corrected him, "I just think he was a little disappointed in me." I told them about our visit to Heaven's House and the conversation we had about getting rid of unnecessary people.

"Well, Tristan, you should talk to him," Kim advised.

"I know I should, but I don't really know how." My other line rang just then. "Guys, I have to go," I said realizing I was still at work.

"Okay, Trey, we will make plans later about getting tested," Kim said before we all disconnected.

I switched to my other line. "This is Tristan," I said.

"Hey, Tristan." It was Monty!

Good looking out, Christy, I thought to myself. Monty had a somber tone to his voice.

"Monty, how are you? Are you okay? I mean . . ." I stammered. I really didn't know what to say.

"I'm okay, Tristan. I'm really not in the mood to be dealing with this kind of stress, but I know I have to." Monty explained that he had spoken to his publicist and had a statement ready for the press.

"Well good," I said to Monty, "because I need you to make a call to V103 and give them a statement."

Monty let out a sigh. "Okay, Tristan, if you say so."

I had Monty hold while I conferenced him in with the manager over at V103. The V103 manager briefed Monty on what was about to take place. The live interview was only going to last a couple of minutes, and the questions would be light. Monty agreed, and before long, we were live on the air. I couldn't believe it; I had butterflies in my stomach like I was the one making the statement.

My job was becoming more and more interesting by the day. I felt very important at this particular moment, like what I was doing was curing world hunger. I pressed the mute button on my phone and listened to the call. Frank Ski introduced Monty.

"This is a V103 exclusive!" he said. "We've got Monty Wilson from the group Exodus on the line with us," Frank said.

"Hey, Monty, baby," Wanda said giggling.

"Don't laugh, Wanda. This is serious," Frank added. "My man, Monty, what's up? Now listen, tell us in your own words what happened last night?" Frank said.

I listened intently as Monty began to tell his side of the story. "Well, Frank," Monty started off sounding cool and confident, "it isn't what everyone is making it out to be."

"Well, tell us how it is," Wanda said.

"I mean I wasn't soliciting sex, and I wasn't acting in a lewd manner," Monty said.

"What were you doing in that park so late at night?" Frank asked. Even I wanted to know the answer to that one.

"I was just taking a walk. I had just finished a performance at a club, and I wanted to get some fresh air. I had a lot on my mind, and I just needed to relax," Monty explained.

"Yeah, you wanted to relax all right," Wanda said laughing. Frank chuckled trying to hold back his laughter.

"Man, we just have one more question for you?" Frank asked.

Okay, I thought, *here we go. He's going to ask him. I just know it.*

"Monty, are you gay?" Frank asked.

He did it! Oh my God. What is Monty going to say?

"Well, Frank, I'm really not at liberty to answer any personal questions because of this pending case. I will say that I do like women. I always have, and I always will." Monty said that like a true professional; however, he really didn't answer the question. If Monty liked women that could mean he was bisexual, or he could've just been lying.

Frank and Wanda thanked Monty for the interview. Frank even gave a little plug for the party in December, and then they were gone. I couldn't tell if Monty was telling the truth or not . . . dishonesty seemed to be going around lately.

CHAPTER 12

Kim

Kim was exhausted. Between dealing with Kevin and his car accident and Rashawn and his cancer, Kim's burden was heavy. She looked to God for strength, but it was getting hard to put on a smile every day and pretend like everything was okay. She was tired of being the strong black woman. When was it going to be her turn to let it all out?

"I guess it won't be today," Kim thought out loud as she made her way up the elevator to the fourth floor of Grady Memorial Hospital. She was paying Kevin his daily visit. Jamal was with her today. She looked down at Jamal who was tightly holding her hand. He had the biggest grin on his face. He was always excited to visit his father. Jamal was the only thing in her life that brought her peace. He was so full of joy and love.

"Mommy, are we there yet?" Jamal said jumping anxiously.

"We're almost there, baby," Kim responded just as the elevator doors opened. Kim led Jamal by the hand down the long corridor to Kevin's room. Kim could hear the sounds of laughter and loud talking just outside Kevin's door. It sounded like Tawanda, Kevin's sister. Kim rolled her eyes. She really couldn't stand Tawanda.

"Aunt TT," Jamal screamed bursting into Kevin's room. Kim followed behind.

"Hey, shawty," Tawanda said scooping Jamal up.

"Hey, Kev. Hi, Tawanda," Kim said.

Tawanda sighed and rolled her eyes at Kim.

"Hey, baby," Kevin said trying to adjust himself in the bed. Kevin was still banged up pretty bad. His left arm was in a cast, and so was his right leg. His face was still swollen, but at least he was on the road to recovery.

"Why is it so dark in here?" Kim said going over to the curtains. She pulled them back letting the sun in.

"Don't be coming in here trying to run shit!" Tawanda said. Kim ignored her.

"Hey, Tawanda, not in front of my boy," Kevin checked her. Kim smiled.

"Shut up, Kevin! Anyways, I'm 'bout to go," Tawanda said as she gathered her things and headed out the door. "Bye, Jamal," she said before leaving.

She is such a bitch, Kim thought to herself. Jamal jumped in the bed with Kevin and began flipping through the channels on the television.

"Daddy, you feel better?" Jamal asked.

"I do now that you here," Kevin said. Kim loved to see Jamal and Kevin interact with each other. Jamal always brought out the softer side of Kevin. Kim took a seat next to Kevin's bed.

"Kevin, I came today because I have something to do in the hospital, and I am going to leave Jamal in here with you while I go handle this business," Kim said.

"What business you got to handle?" Kevin asked sounding a bit jealous.

Kim explained how she and her friends were getting tested to donate bone marrow for Rashawn.

"Aww, man, I'm sorry to hear that," Kevin said.

Tyler was supposed to be meeting Kim in about ten minutes on the first floor to get tested. "Jamal, you be good. I'm only going to be gone for a few minutes," Kim said.

"Okay, mommy. I'll take care of daddy for you," he said. Kim smiled; her heart felt warm thinking of Kevin and Jamal. Kim stopped at the nurse's station and informed them she was going to be on the first floor for a few minutes and asked them to keep an eye on Jamal. The nurses loved Jamal. He was definitely a ladies' man, so they eagerly obliged. Kim headed downstairs to the oncology department where she met with Tyler.

"Hey, honey," Tyler greeted Kim. They embraced and then took a seat in the waiting area. Both of them had butterflies in their stomachs. Kim said a silent prayer for at least one of them to be a match. "Where's Tristan?" Tyler said.

"He's working. You know he's got a lot on his hands since that story broke about Monty Wilson," Kim said. "I think he's going to come on his own. What about Eric?"

"You know he's here at the hospital now. I think he's working all day today," Tyler said. "Maybe we should go see him when we are done," he continued.

Kim shook her head in agreement. They sat together waiting on the doctor. "Kimberly Freeman," a pudgy nurse said a few moments later.

Kim looked up. "That's me, but what about my friend here," Kim motioned toward Tyler.

"We'll call him in a minute," she responded in a huffy tone.

Kim looked back at Tyler and rolled her eyes. *I know this bitch ain't got no attitude when my friend is dying,* Kim thought to herself. She wanted to say it out loud but didn't.

Kim followed the nurse to an examiner's room where she was asked to take a seat and roll up her sleeves. Kim obliged. "The doctor will be with you in a moment," the rude nurse said before shutting the door and leaving Kim in the room alone.

As Kim sat there waiting on the doctor, she reflected on everything that had happened. She just couldn't believe Rashawn had cancer. She tried to be optimistic, but she knew Rashawn didn't look good at all. He had very little energy, and she could tell this was serious. She also thought about Kevin. Since he came out of his coma, he was a different man, and Kim liked it. The pastor from Kevin's church came by on a regular basis to pray and witness to Kevin, and he seemed to be taking heed, even quoting scriptures to Kim. Then there was Brandon. She wasn't spending much time with him, but she didn't mind. Brandon was beginning to act very strange. He was lovely to be around, but he was so hard to track down, and she still had yet to see where he lived. Kim had a strong female intuition, so when it became increasingly difficult to reach Brandon, she just let it be, although she did miss him from time to time. The brother did know how to satisfy a woman. But there needed to be more to a relationship then just great sex, and Kim knew this. The doctor came in shortly and interrupted Kim's thoughts.

The whole process was rather seamless. He drew some blood from her and explained about the test and sent her on her way. If she was a match, she would be notified. Although it was highly unlikely she was a match, it didn't hurt to try. Kim said another little prayer as she made her way back to the lobby where she found Tyler was still waiting.

"Tyler, they still haven't called you back?"

"Child, yes! I done gave my blood and had my way with the doctor all in under fifteen minutes," Tyler snapped his fingers in the air.

Kim laughed. "Come on, boy. Let's go see Eric." Kim grabbed Tyler by the arm and pulled him toward the door.

Eric worked in admissions, so Kim and Tyler headed that way. There was an older woman sitting at the front desk in admissions when they got there. Her name tag read Eleanor.

"Hi, Eleanor," Kim said walking up to the front counter.

The elderly woman looked up and smiled flashing a mouth full of dentures. "Yes, ma'am, can I help you?" she said.

"Yes, is Eric available?" Kim asked smiling back.

Eleanor pointed towards a sitting area by the entry way. "He's over there, sweetie," she replied.

Kim and Tyler looked in the direction the lady was pointing. There was Eric, sitting down with his back towards them so he didn't see Kim or Tyler. He was talking to a woman. The woman looked very familiar to Kim. It seemed that they were in a deep conversation. Tyler started to make his way towards Eric, but Kim stopped him. She grabbed Tyler by the arm and pulled him around the corner.

"What did you do that for girl?" Tyler said. The admissions area was very busy; people were walking around asking for directions. They were checking in and out, so it was noisy. Kim pulled Tyler towards the elevator. They got on and headed back to the fourth floor. Once on the elevator Kim finally started to talk.

"Don't you recognize that woman Eric was talking to?" Kim asked.

"No, honey, who is she?" Tyler responded.

"Remember in church when Tristan said a woman was staring at him, and when he asked her who she was she ran off?"

"So what?" Tyler replied

"Well, obviously, she knows Eric, and he didn't even say anything. Isn't that strange?" Kim said.

"Girl, you are too dramatic? That's what this is about?" Tyler said as they got off the elevator and headed towards Kevin's room.

"I don't know, Tyler . . . something ain't right about that," Kim said making a face.

G. L. Johnson

Kim and Tyler entered Kevin's room where they found both Kevin and Jamal fast asleep. Jamal was lying next to Kevin as they snored. Kim smiled as she walked over and kissed Jamal on the forehead.

"Well, I'm going to go back downstairs to see Eric," Tyler said.

"Find out who that woman is?" Kim said as she waved goodbye and took her seat next to Kevin's bed.

CHAPTER 13

Eric

Eric was in a slump. He was tired of his job, he never had enough money, and he was lonely. He was working his butt off at the hospital in hopes of getting a promotion, and they ended up giving the position to someone else. His love life was in the toilet as well. Eric had been in a long-term relationship, but it had ended nearly six months ago. The guy dumped Eric because he was too controlling. Eric longed for someone to love, so when Tristan came to town, he just knew he had found it. Too bad Tristan didn't feel the same way. Eric would put on his best game for Tristan, only to have Tristan dismiss him every time. Who the hell did Tristan think he was? He wasn't all that. He was fine and all, but so was Eric.

Eric was a very troubled man. He grew up in Seattle, Washington, raised by his mother and father who were very strict Jehovah's Witnesses. When it became clear that Eric was gay, his father forced him to go to Bible retreats that were supposed to heal him of homosexuality. Little did Eric's father know, this is where he had his first homosexual encounter. One of the group leaders, a man well in his twenties, engaged in sexual encounters with Eric on numerous occasions, even though Eric was only thirteen. At sixteen when Eric still had not been "cured" of homosexuality, his father kicked him out the house, and he was sent to live in Atlanta with his aunt on his mother's side. Since then Eric really didn't have relationship with either of his parents. Now at twenty-six, it had been ten years since he had even seen his parents. Eric, however, had kept in touch with his older sisters, Jeanette and Lisa.

Jeanette, a school teacher in Seattle, would always send money to Eric and often came and visited him. She was front and center when he graduated from high school; Jeanette was more of a mother figure than his real mother ever was. Lisa, who is just two years older than Eric, would often call but never came to visit. Lisa had gotten married a few years back. She tried to get Eric to come to the wedding, but he refused since he knew his parents would be there. Because he skipped the wedding, Eric had never met his brother-in-law. He had seen pictures but had never met him in person.

Recently, Lisa's husband had gotten a job in Atlanta, so the two of them packed up and moved from Seattle to Georgia. This was good for Eric because he missed his sister. They had always been so much alike as kids, and he loved having family close. Lisa turned out to be a hassle for Eric though. In just under a year, she'd managed to drive Eric crazy.

Her husband was always causing drama in her life. He would cheat on her constantly, sometimes staying gone for days at a time. Eric tried to persuade Lisa to leave him, but she was in love. She would often become delusional when it came to her husband, and she always remained secretive. In fact since they had been living in Atlanta, Eric still hadn't met her husband. Whenever Eric would come by the house, he was never there. Eric was beginning to think he didn't exist. Then one day Lisa came to him and said she was pregnant.

"Wow, Lisa, this is good!" Eric said excited he would have a niece or nephew.

"No, Eric, it's not. I think Brandon is cheating on me again," Lisa said as she started to cry. Brandon was Lisa's husband. From the pictures Eric saw he was very attractive and well built; he could see why women were falling over themselves to be with him. Lisa was hysterical. She wanted to save her marriage at any cost. Eric recalled the look in her eyes as she pleaded with Eric to help her. Eric hated to see his sister in so much pain, so he vowed to himself that he would help her.

Of course Eric was shocked when he saw Brandon embraced in a passionate hug with Kim at the hospital the day Kevin was in the car accident. Eric didn't know what to do. He wanted to tell Lisa, but he was scared for Kim. He wasn't sure how Lisa would react. So he sat on this information. Lisa had been investigating on her own; however, and Eric didn't think she knew anything about Kim. In fact it surprised him when Lisa came back with a name of whom she thought Brandon was seeing . . . . Tristan!

This is impossible, Eric thought to himself. Lisa was furious of course. She couldn't believe her husband was sleeping with another man. Eric couldn't believe that the other man was Tristan, but he recalled the night Tristan met his mystery date at Bulldogs. Eric hadn't really paid much attention to him. He had been so worried about Tristan, he didn't really get a good look at the mystery man, but it all made sense. Tristan's friend went by the name of BJ, and Lisa's husband's name was Brandon Jackson. Everything was coming together.

Eric had all the answers; he was the only person who knew that Kim and Tristan were dating the same person, someone who just happened to be married to his sister. Any decent person who had this information would have told the respective parties, but not Eric. He was already mad with Tristan for not giving him the time of day, so he decided to sit on the information. Lisa came to Eric one day and insisted Eric find information on Tristan, so Eric broke down and told her he knew Tristan. He left out Kim for some reason. Lisa was even more infuriated. She demanded to meet Tristan, but Eric had other plans. He wanted to get back at Tristan.

To appease Lisa, he told her to come to their church when he knew Tristan would be there. Lisa was instructed not to speak to Tristan at all. She was okay with this for now. Eric thought it was all going to blow up in his face when Tristan stopped Lisa in the church vestibule thinking that he recognized her, but Lisa made a quick get away.

Lisa was growing more and more weary of playing games with Tristan and Brandon. This particular day, she'd had just about enough, so she went to Eric's job at the hospital. Lisa wanted Eric to know that she was fed up. Lisa stormed into Grady Memorial Hospital on a rampage.

"May I speak to Eric?" she demanded from the kind elderly lady sitting behind the desk. Eleanor picked up the phone and dialed a few numbers and before long she was talking to Eric. Eric was in the back processing paperwork for newly admitted patients.

"Eric, you have a visitor," Eleanor said once Eric picked up the phone.

"Who is it?" Eric asked.

Eleanor in turn asked for Lisa's name. "My name is Lisa. I'm his sister. Now tell him to get his ass out here!" she demanded.

Eric could hear Lisa sounding off on the other end. "I'll be right out, Eleanor. I'm so sorry," Eric said as he rushed out of the office to the front admissions area.

"Lisa, what is wrong with you?" he demanded grabbing her arm and pulling her towards the waiting area. "This is my job! You can't be acting like this!"

Lisa started to cry. Her tears rolled down her face like pellets.

"What's wrong, Lisa? Is it the baby?" Eric asked fearing the worst. Lisa was barely showing. With her tiny frame, she would have to tell you before you knew she was pregnant.

"No, Eric. Nothing's wrong with the baby. I've just had enough of this bullshit," she said. "Now I'm going to have to take matters into my own hands." The look in her eyes was demented. She was a woman scorned, and she was ready for revenge.

"Calm down. What do you think you are going to do, Lisa? You have got to think about the baby," Eric said trying to get Lisa under control. *It wasn't time yet,* Eric thought. *Tristan hadn't suffered enough.*

"Well, I am thinking about my baby. That's why I put Brandon out," Lisa proclaimed. "I found out he's been renting an apartment in College Park. That faggot probably been taking Tristan there," she said.

The word faggot cut Eric like a knife. His father used to call him that. "Lisa, don't use that word," he said.

"I'm sorry, Eric, but I can't take this. I told Brandon to get out because I knew his ass was cheating."

"And what did he say?" Eric asked.

"He didn't say shit. What could he say?" Lisa said. "He moved the rest of his stuff this morning."

"Well, Lisa, you have to calm down! Go home, and I'll be over there when I get off," Eric instructed as he escorted her to the main entrance.

"Eric, what are we going to do?" she asked looking helpless.

"We'll think of something," Eric said. He gave her a hug goodbye and sent her on her way. He headed back to the office to finish his work.

"Eric, you had some other visitors," Eleanor said as he walked past her.

"Who?" he asked looking confused.

"I don't know, a girl and a guy. They walked off when they saw you talking to your sister."

"What did they look like?" Eric pressed.

"Well, the woman was dark skinned and very beautiful, and the fella was a little on the chunky side, but attractive as well," she said smiling eager to play private eye.

Eleanor was the sweetest person Eric had ever met, but she could also be a mess. She loved to gossip, and her position at the front desk gave her a bird's eye view of what was going on at the hospital at all times. She was the first to know that Eric was up for a promotion, and she was the first to know that he didn't get it. Eleanor, now in her sixties, thrived on drama and loved taking part in any investigative work. Eleanor was the one who exposed the affair between the hospital administrator and the head nurse in the neonatal department. So Eric knew if it was information he needed, Eleanor was the person to go to. He also knew that if there was a secret that needed to be kept, then he needed to stay as far away from Eleanor as possible.

Based off the description that Eleanor gave Eric knew exactly who it was that had come by to see him, Kim and Tyler. They must have been there to get tested for Rashawn's bone marrow transplant. Eric prayed they didn't recognize Lisa. He went back in the office and shut the door and began typing a note that he would deliver after work.

CHAPTER 14

Tristan

I was completely worn out. This scandal with Monty had taken its toll on me. I had begged and pleaded with just about every sponsor to not pull out. Most of them were okay, but I did lose one account. I worked so late I didn't even realize that it was already eight o'clock in the evening. I had just finished setting the date of the event for December tenth. The club owner wanted to push for a time after Christmas, but I held my ground, and we were booked for the tenth. I had been working so hard I didn't notice that I hadn't seen Michael all day. *Wow, he must really be upset with me.*

I packed up my things and headed out the office. It was very quiet since everyone had already left for the day. I headed towards my car eager to get home. As I got my keys out, I noticed there was a note on my windshield.

Not another one, I thought feeling aggravated. This was starting to piss me off. I snatched the note off the windshield and read it:

You lie down with dogs
You wake up with fleas
Be careful of the strangers you make as bed fellows

I folded up the note and stuffed it in my pocket. I was going to save this one for future reference. I needed to get to the bottom of this, and I wasn't going to let whoever this was get the best of me. I hopped in my car and sped home.

Michael was home when I got there. He was sitting on the sofa flipping through channels. He looked as if he had just finished working out. He had on his workout gear and was still wet with sweat. He looked marvelous.

"Hi, Michael," I said kicking my shoes off at the door.

"Hey," Michael said unenthusiastically.

I sighed. I guess he still had an attitude with me. I walked over to him and took a seat. The air was thick with tension. "Michael, I think we should talk," I said feeling nervous.

"Yeah, man, we should."

"I know you were a little shocked to find someone in my bed," I said. "I mean I guess we never talked about me having company."

Michael fidgeted in his seat; clearly, I was making him uncomfortable. "I guess I wasn't expecting to see some cat up in your bed, but I should not have been in your space though," he said. "Maybe it would be best if you started looking for an apartment," he blurted out.

What?!?! I was being kicked out again. My mouth fell to the floor. Michael must have realized how shocked I was.

"I mean no rush, Tristan, but maybe you need your own spot. This wasn't supposed to be a permanent fix for you anyways," he said. "Besides I really don't know if I can handle all this."

What did he mean he didn't know if he could handle all of this? Handle what? "Michael, I don't understand," I said as tears began to well up in my eyes.

"Tristan, you still my boy and all," Michael added.

I couldn't believe what I was hearing. I guess it was a bad idea for me to move into Michael's place from the beginning.

"I'm not saying you need to move out today. I'm just saying you should start looking."

Nothing Michael was saying was making me feel better. I got up from my seat and headed towards my room. "That's fine, Michael. I'll move out," I said as I tried my best to hold back my tears. I shut my door and fell face first onto the bed.

I wanted to just lay there forever. Everything was going wrong. Atlanta was not what I thought it would be. My cell phone vibrated in my pocket. It was a number I didn't recognize, so I let it go to voicemail. A few seconds later my phone was beeping to let me know I had a message. I called to check the message.

"Yo, Tristan, it's BJ. Call me when you get this message. My number is 404-555-1379. I need to see you."

Oh wow! BJ finally gave me his private number. I saved the message, but I didn't call him back. Instead, I called my mother.

"Tristan, baby, what's wrong?" my mother said over the phone. I was lying across my bed still in my work clothes sobbing. My mother could always tell when something wasn't right with me.

"Mom, he's putting me out," I said.

"What do you mean, baby? What happened?"

I explained what happened that morning and how Michael felt it was time for me to move out.

"Well, baby, you knew it was only temporary. Right, Tristan?" my mother had a way of always telling me the truth without hurting my feelings.

"I know, Ma, but I don't know if I'm ready to move just yet," I said being honest.

"How about I come out there and help you find an apartment? I really think you need to see your mother anyway," she said.

I immediately smiled; of course I wanted to see my mother. I was already making plans in my head. "Oh please, Ma! When can you come?" I asked wishing she could be with me now.

"Well, I can call the airline and maybe get a flight after Labor Day weekend," she said.

I had forgotten Labor Day was coming up. I was so self-involved that I didn't even know what day it was. Labor Day was a big weekend for black, gay men in Atlanta. That was the weekend that everyone came from all over the country to express their inner gayness. Labor Day weekend allows suppressed men a chance to let it all hang out . . . literally. There would be tons of parties and plenty of gorgeous men just flooding the city ready to snatch off their shirts at any given moment. This was a chance for me to relax and have some fun.

"Okay, mom. It's settled. You can come down the weekend after Labor Day." I said feeling much better.

"Okay, Tristan, I'll call the airline in the morning. Don't you worry. Everything will be fine," she said. I said goodbye to my mother and got ready for bed.

I was supposed to be at the hospital the next morning to get tested for the bone marrow transplant for Rashawn. I was excited to help. Kim said Rashawn health was steadily deteriorating, and I really wanted to do something for him. After I showered, I got on my knees and prayed before jumping into bed. I was in dreamland before I knew it.

I woke up early the next morning; it was Friday, the official kick-off day for Labor Day weekend. I had decided to take the day off. I called Yvette and told her I would be in the field all day, but really I was going to be starting my weekend early. I had an appointment at the doctor's office at 8:30 a.m. I wanted to go in early and get it over with. I hated hospitals.

I woke up to the smell of fresh bacon and eggs. It reminded me of living with Rashawn. Rashawn always had breakfast waiting on me when I woke up. I got out of bed and opened my curtains. The sun flooded in, illuminating my room. The rays from the sun felt good on my skin. I was excited to start my day. I pulled on my wool housecoat and slippers and went into the kitchen.

I found Michael slaving over the kitchen stove. There was bacon, eggs, toast, juice, and grapefruit, the whole works. A gorgeous man that could cook . . . that was hard to come by. He was sure going to make some woman really happy. I yawned, sleep still looming over me.

"Wake up, sleepyhead," Michael said. He was acting as if nothing happened the day before.

"What's all this?" I said still a little upset with him.

"Breakfast. What does it look like?" he said giving me a coy smile.

"Michael, don't be cooking for me because you feel bad about kicking me out," I said tasting a slice of bacon.

"I didn't kick you out, Tristan; I just said you need to start looking. Now sit down and eat," he said.

I smiled; at least our friendship wasn't damaged. I cherished my friendship with Michael. I felt like I could tell him anything, and he wouldn't judge me. I sat at the breakfast bar while he fixed my plate. I was starving, and the food was so good.

"So, are we carpooling today?" Michael asked.

"Well, I'm not going into the office today," I said. I told Michael about going to get tested for Rashawn's bone marrow transplant.

"Well, that's a good idea," Michael said. "You mind if I join you?"

"Sure," I said gobbling up the last of my bacon. *Why was Michael being so nice?* I didn't know what he had up his sleeves, but I brushed it off. I liked Michael like this.

"Maybe later we could swing by Heaven's House and visit the kids?" he added.

That was actually a good idea. Besides, I had promised Alicia I would come back to visit. I finished up my meal and retreated back in my room to get dressed. Before long, Michael and I were in my car headed to Grady Memorial. For some reason I was a little nervous.

"What are you so jumpy for?" Michael asked.

"I don't know. I think I'm a little nervous," I admitted.

Once we were inside the hospital, we found the oncology department. There was a plump nurse sitting behind the reception area. "Can I help you?" she said with a slight attitude.

I walked up to her, "Um, yes, I have an appointment."

"Name?" she said cutting me off.

"Um, Tristan Smith."

"Okay. Have a seat, Mr. Smith."

I looked back at Michael; he gave me a puzzled look. "Well, ma'am, I also wanted to see if my friend here could get tested," I said.

The nurse let out a loud sigh to indicate she was irritated with me. "What's his name?"

"His name is Michael Washington," I said.

"All right, we'll call him shortly. If both of you could take a seat," she said motioning to the chairs up against the wall.

Boy was she rude, I thought to myself as we sat. Michael and I began flipping through magazines. About five minutes had passed when the door to the oncology office opened and in walked Eric. I was a little surprised to see him even though I knew he worked in the hospital.

"Hey, Eric," I said smiling.

Eric gave me a strange look before saying hello. "What up, Tristan?" he said. "I didn't know you were going to be here today," he said looking at Michael.

"Hello, Eric. Good to see you again," Michael said extending his hand.

Eric returned the favor. "You here to get tested too?" Eric asked Michael.

"Yeah, man," Michael replied.

"Mr. Smith," the nurse called my name.

"Well, guys, that's me," I said. I got up and followed the nurse to the back where I was instructed to roll up my sleeve and have a seat. The process took all of ten minutes, and the hospital stated they would notify me if I was a match.

I went back to the lobby where I found Michael and Eric still sitting where I'd left them. The nurse called Michael's name next. As he followed the nurse to the back, I sat down next to Eric.

"So what do you have planned for this weekend?" I asked Eric making small talk.

"Nothing really," he said looking down at the floor. He never really looked up at me, but today he was acting even weirder.

"Eric, is everything all right?"

"Yeah, I'm good," he mumbled still looking at the ground.

"Well, Tyler said he wanted to go to the pool party tomorrow," I said recalling the conversation I'd had with Tyler that morning. He had called me to invite me to his place to meet a few of his friends from out of town that night and to a big pool party at the host hotel tomorrow.

"Yeah, I'll probably be going," Eric said. Michael came out just then.

"Well, Eric, we have to go. See you later," I said looking puzzled.

Once we were back in the car, Michael and I headed to Heaven's House. "Your friend is a little strange," Michael blurted out as we made our way through traffic.

"What do you mean?" I said.

"I don't really know, but something doesn't sit right with me about him." Michael sounded serious.

"Well, what did you guys talk about?" I asked.

"It's not really what he said. It's how he was acting," Michael explained.

I agreed with Michael. Eric was acting strange. But I let it go. I really didn't feel like dealing with Eric and his issues.

"All I'm saying is just be careful, Tristan," Michael said as we pulled up to Heaven's House.

I was excited to spend time with Alicia. She had really struck accord with me. Tracy greeted us at the door. "Hey, Tracy," I said giving her a hug. She had her usual bright smile.

"Hi, honey. Welcome!" she said showing us in.

"Where's Tosha?" I said looking around. The reception area was empty.

"Well, she has class on Friday mornings, so she won't be in until this afternoon," Tracy said.

"How are the kids?" Michael asked.

"Well . . ." Tracy's voice trailed off as she got a somber look on her face.

Oh no. Something bad has happened. My mind immediately went to Alicia. *Oh, God, I hope nothing happened to her.*

"It's about José, Michael," Tracy continued.

"Is he okay?" Michael asked.

"He went into a coma last night and passed away this morning."

"Oh no," Michael said as tears began to swell up in his eyes.

"Yeah, the kids are pretty shook up about it," Tracy added. Tracy informed me that José had lupus. He was fourteen years old and very well liked at Heaven's House. All the little kids loved him, but he was very ill. Michael would often pick José up and take him to a baseball game or the mall. José's parents both were incarcerated, and he didn't have any other family who was able to care for him properly. That's how he ended up at Heaven's House. Tracy went to Michael and gave him a hug. I was shocked but relieved that it wasn't Alicia at the same time.

I found Alicia out back sitting on a swing, her little feet dangling above the ground. "Tristan! You came back!" she said jumping off the swing running to me. She jumped into my arms giving me the biggest hug.

"Of course I came back, missy. Didn't I promise you?" I said giving her a little tickle on the tummy.

"My friend died today," Alicia said in a somber tone. Her big brown eyes had sadness in them that reached into my soul. I got a little chocked up. Why should this precious little girl have to endure so much pain in her life?

"I heard," I said. "I'm so sorry to hear that, Alicia. Are you okay?" I really didn't know what to say to her. I wanted to say everything was going to be fine, but that would be lying.

"I want to swing," Alicia suddenly proclaimed as she jumped out of my arms and ran to the swing set. Kids had a way of forgetting about their problems. I wish I could do that. I pushed her gently as she kicked her legs in the air. She screamed with glee as she went higher and higher. Her laughter was intoxicating, and soon, I was laughing as well. A few of the other kids joined us, and we were all having a good time outside in the sun. We played tag, hide and seek, and kickball. The kids ran until they didn't have a drop of energy left.

"Alicia," I said after a round of tag. I had fallen out in the grass pooped. "I think it's time for me to go," I said.

She smiled at me. "Okay," she replied just as simple as that. That little girl had the weight of the world on her shoulders, but she wore a smile every time I saw her. She was truly my hero. I gave her a hug before we located Michael inside playing chess with one of the older boys.

"Hey, Michael, are you ready to go?" I asked looking at my watch. I had tons of things to do, and I needed to get started, although I would have loved to stay for a little while longer.

"Yeah, I guess," Michael replied. He turned to the boy he was playing chess with. "Billy, I have to go, but I'll be back really soon, man. Keep your head up." The boy looked up from the chessboard and mustarded a slight grin. "He's pretty shook up about José," Michael said. "They were like best friends."

I sighed. Death was such a horrible thing. I thought about Rashawn. I really needed to reach out to him. Kim said he seemed to be getting weaker and weaker. I just prayed one of us would be a match for him.

"What are you thinking about?" Michael asked as we made our way back to the apartment. Michael needed to get his car because he was going into the office, and I was supposed to be going shopping. It must have been obvious that I was deep in thought.

"Ummm, nothing," I said jumping back into reality.

"Oh come on, Tristan. I know you have something on your mind."

"I'm just thinking about Rashawn. I feel so bad for him," I said being earnest.

"Well, Tristan, do something about it."

"It's not that easy."

"Really it is, Tristan."

At that moment, I was pulling into the parking lot. As Michael got out the car, he turned to me and said, "Tristan, you make things hard on yourself." And with that he was off.

Was Michael right? Was I making things more difficult than they should be?

CHAPTER 15

Brandon

Brandon sat in his empty, one bedroom apartment alone in the dark. It was a bright, sunny Friday outside, but he had all the curtains drawn. He was upset; his life had suddenly spun out of control. He had been renting this one bedroom apartment in College Park for a couple of months now. His wife knew nothing about it, or so he thought.

Brandon and his wife, Lisa, shared a three bedroom home in East Point not far from College Park. It was just the two of them, but they wanted a large home in hopes of creating a family. They had moved to Atlanta because Brandon had gotten a job offer he couldn't refuse. In Seattle, Brandon and Lisa had what you would call a perfect life, well, from the outside looking in. They met at church; she was the pastor's daughter and fly as ever. It took a minute for him to reel her in, but once he had her, she was hooked. They dated for a while before he asked her to marry him. They had a big wedding in the summer. Both seemed to be so happy, but Brandon had a problem.

Brandon constantly cheated on Lisa; he'd probably slept with almost every woman in Seattle and the surrounding areas. At first, Lisa didn't know, and when she found out she pretended not to know. However, once Brandon started bringing home STDs like gonorrhea, Lisa started to clown. She wanted to leave him, but she loved Brandon so much. So when the offer came to move to Atlanta, Lisa eagerly jumped at the opportunity. She was ready for the change and tired of having to fight women in Seattle over her husband.

Brandon was ready for a change as well. He'd had enough of Seattle women and welcomed the challenge the southern women would bring. He'd heard about how freaky the down south ladies were. However, the move to Atlanta had proven not to be a good idea. Once Brandon was let loose in Atlanta, he was like a mad man, having his way with every woman he could. Then one day he got a taste of something new.

One night Brandon was pissy drunk walking down Peachtree Street trying to find his car. Amidst his search, he stumbled upon a club called Bulldogs. Now residents of Atlanta all know that Bulldogs is a happening place for black, gay men. Being that Brandon wasn't a native of Atlanta, along with the fact that he was sloppy drunk, he didn't have a clue. So Brandon, deciding to have one last drink before heading home to his wife, went in.

Brandon stumbled through the front door; the music was pumping loudly, making his body vibrate. As he made his way through the crowd, his manhood started to grow; he was hornier than ever. He thought he would have his drink then go home and tear into his wife. That proved to be a moot thought. Once at the bar, he ordered a shot of tequila and drank it down in two seconds.

"Hey, sexy," a deep voice whispered into his ear just as he was placing the empty shot glass on the bar. Brandon shook his head confused. Did he hear correctly? It sounded like a man whispering in his ear. Brandon turned around, and there was an attractive black man smiling back at him. He was wearing a tank top that showed off his massive muscles. He had just as many muscles as Brandon, if not more. Brandon pushed the strange man away.

"Man, I ain't gay!" Brandon said pissed off.

"Well, what are you doing in here?" the man shot back.

Brandon looked around and noticed there was not a single sista in the building. Yet, there were men all over dancing and grinding against each other. "What the hell!" Brandon shouted. Brandon started to storm out of the bar, but the strange man was persistent. He followed Brandon.

"Man, I told you I'm not gay!" Brandon turned to him and said.

"I can't tell," the man said looking down at Brandon's manhood which was still at full attention. Before Brandon knew it, the man had his tongue deep in Brandon's mouth. Brandon started to pull away, but fireworks began to go off in his body. He didn't know if it was the liquor, but he enjoyed the kiss. It didn't take long before they were headed to the strange man's house and engaged in full out man on man sex.

Brandon had never had sex so good. And just that quickly, he was addicted. Brandon made several trips to Bulldogs; he would hook up with men and have meaningless sex using the name BJ. That's when he decided to get the apartment. He didn't want to bring men home to his wife's bed. It was bad enough he was bringing women there.

Brandon did feel bad, however, about sleeping with men. He was tormented by the fact that he liked it so much. He even blamed Lisa in a desperate attempt to justify what he was doing, saying she wasn't able to satisfy him. This was why he continued to date women. He met Kim, a beautiful hairdresser; he thought she would keep him from wanting men. Kim was perfect, except for her crazy baby daddy. She was just what he needed. Then he met Tristan.

Tristan was gorgeous, funny, and sexy. Tristan turned Brandon's world inside out. Brandon craved Tristan; soon he'd cut off all the women he was dealing with, including Kim, just to be with Tristan. Every free moment he had, he wanted to be with Tristan.

His wife, Lisa, however, was getting weary of Brandon's infidelity. This is why Brandon found himself alone in his apartment. Lisa had put him out. She had recently announced she was pregnant, much to Brandon's dismay, and she was sick of him cheating, so he had to go. He couldn't be sure if she knew about Tristan, but he knew he was becoming sloppier with his cover-ups. At that moment, he sat in his apartment craving Tristan. He picked up the phone and dialed Tristan's number. It went straight to voicemail. "Tristan, this is BJ. I need to see you, man. Call me when you get this."

Brandon had plenty of other chickenheads he could call: men and women. But he wanted Tristan. Brandon thought for a moment before coming to the realization that he was in love with Tristan. The thought of being in love with another man didn't sit very well with Brandon. He was a ladies' man at heart, but there was something about Tristan.

Brandon sat there pondering what he should do. He was literally starving for a taste of Tristan's sweet nectar. His pager went off. It was Lisa. Brandon ignored the page. He was not in the mood to deal with Lisa. He needed to find Tristan.

CHAPTER 16

Kim

$\mathcal{T}$he hair salon was packed. It was the start of Labor Day weekend and everyone wanted fresh hairdos. Kim had five clients back to back all before noon, and there were several walk-ins to attend to. Kim didn't mind the added work. She needed the money, and it took away from the stress of her life.

She had recently gotten a call from the doctor informing her that she was not a match for Rashawn. When she told Rashawn, he didn't seem the least bit bothered. He said he expected she wouldn't be a match.

On a good note, Kevin was healing wonderfully. He had a whole new attitude, really getting into the Bible. He read the Bible a lot while he lay in his hospital bed. The doctors said he would be going home soon, but he would need physical therapy and supervision at home. Kevin was eager to leave the hospital, but he didn't want to go to his mother's house. He wanted to stay with Kim; however, Kim wasn't so sure about this arrangement. She was happy he was doing well, but she was trying to move on with her life. She promised Kevin she would think about it.

She could use Kevin's company since Brandon was now completely missing in action. The last time they had spent anytime together, Brandon had sexed her down and left in a haste. He left her to feeling cheap and used. Kim didn't like feeling like a whore, so she didn't bother calling him, and he hadn't called her. She wasn't sure she even wanted him to call. It was too bad. Until then, Brandon had seemed so perfect, but Kim knew nothing was ever how it seemed.

Kim's next client for the day was Yolanda. Yolanda was one of her good friends whom she had grown up with. She was completely ghetto fabulous with long weave, long nails, and clothes that were always too tight. She was definitely what the men would call a "brick house." Kim didn't know how Yolanda had landed the job at OneStop Event's as the receptionist, especially since she had never had a real job in her life. Yolanda was the kind of girl who relied on men to take care of her. Most of the time she dated drug dealers and hustlers, and none of them seemed to mind paying her bills.

"Yolanda, come here," Kim said motioning for Yolanda to sit in her chair. Yolanda was flirting with one of the barbers.

"Girl, here I come," she said as she sauntered over wearing a tight miniskirt and high heels. Kim tossed a styling cape around Yolanda and proceeded to work her magic. "So, girl, what's up with your boy Tristan?" Yolanda asked ready to gossip.

"What do you mean?" Kim asked.

"Girl, somebody is stalking ole boy. They've been sending letters to the job, calling and hanging up, and everything," Yolanda said.

Kim frowned. "He's still getting those notes?" Kim asked rhetorically.

"Oh, so you knew about it?" Yolanda replied.

"Yeah, I knew, but I didn't think he was still getting them." This didn't sit well with Kim. She was afraid for Tristan.

"Sounds like your boy is in some trouble, and I don't think he even realizes it."

Kim thought about Tristan as she styled Yolanda's hair. Who could be sending these notes and why? She remembered the woman from church. For some reason that woman stuck in Kim's head. She knew it was the same person Eric had been talking to.

"Girl, you're always put a hurtin' on this head of mine," Yolanda said admiring herself in the mirror once Kim finished. "I would stay and chat, but I have to get back to work. I'll holla, girl," Yolanda said handing Kim $50. Kim collected the money, but before she moved to her next client she dialed Tyler's number from her cell phone.

"Hey, Kim," Tyler said. There was a lot of noise in the background.

"Boy, what's going on over there?" Kim asked.

"Oh, I have a people in town for the weekend. You should come over tonight," he said.

"No, I have to see about Kevin," Kim said. She really wasn't in the mood to be in a room full of gorgeous men, none of which would be interested in her. Besides her little group of friends was enough. "I was calling to see if you talked to Eric that day at the hospital?" Kim asked.

"You know I didn't. I ended up leaving, and I forgot all about it. He's supposed to be coming by tonight. I'll ask him then," Tyler said. "You must be really worried about Tristan."

Kim didn't say anything, but she was worried. Before getting off the phone, Tyler told Kim the doctor had called and said he wasn't a match for Rashawn.

"They called me today," he said.

Kim sighed. If it wasn't one thing, it was another. She hung up and began to tend to her client.

CHAPTER 17

Tristan

"So you'll be here next Friday?" I was on the phone with my mother. She was calling to tell me she had booked a flight for next weekend.

"Yes, sweetie, so I need you to pick me up from the airport. You know your momma hasn't been to too many places."

My mother was not well-traveled. Nebraska was her home, and that was that. I smiled. I couldn't wait for her to arrive in Atlanta. "Well, I'll be there waiting for you, Momma."

"Okay, baby. Well, I have to go. Your Aunt Elaine is coming by. We're going shopping today to find me some traveling clothes."

I laughed. My mother could be so country sometimes. "Okay, Momma. Love you."

I was getting ready to head out to Tyler's house. He was having a get together with his out of town friends. The day had been a long one, and it was time to unwind. I had been to the doctor, visited the kids at Heaven's House, gone shopping, and even went into work for a bit. We'd had a last minute staff meeting, and it was required that I be there. Now I was dressed and ready to party.

I grabbed my keys before giving myself the once over in the mirror. As I headed out the front door, I bumped into Michael who was coming in. "Oh, Michael," I said catching a whiff of his cologne. He always smelled so good.

"What up, Tristan? You headed out?" he said.

"Yeah, I'm going over to Tyler's."

"Well, Tristan, be careful," Michael said with a concerned look on his face.

"Michael, you sound as if I'm going into a battlefield or something."

"Just be careful."

"Okay," I replied and headed to the elevator. As I walked to my car, my cell phone went off. It was BJ again. I ignored his call. Tonight was going to be about me. I hopped in my car and headed out to Tyler's.

Tyler's apartment was small and packed to capacity. It seemed every queen from across the nation had made there way to Tyler's place. I squeezed through the front door making my way to the kitchen where I knew I would find Tyler. Sure enough, he was standing over the stove frying up some chicken wings.

"Hey, baby," Tyler said greeting me with a smile. There were several other people milling around the kitchen. Ironically, everyone that was in the kitchen was of the plus-size persuasion.

"Wow, Tyler, this place is packed! How do you know all of these people?" I asked.

"Honey, I don't know half them folks in there. You know word spreads, and when there's free liquor, the girls will turn up."

"Tyler, he's cute," said one of the plus-sized boys looking at me with lustful eyes.

"Oh, honey, he is taken," Tyler shot back winking at me. Although I wasn't taken, Tyler knew I was not interested in anyone in that kitchen.

"Honey, go mingle," Tyler told me. "Have some fun. I think Eric is out there somewhere," Tyler said as he pushed me out the kitchen. I wasn't the type to just go up to strangers and start a conversation, so I headed to the liquor to make a drink.

I was enjoying a nice vodka and orange juice and talking to a cute boy from New York when my cell phone rang. I answered without even looking at the caller ID.

"Hello," I said trying to plug my right ear to shield the noise.

"Man, Tristan, why you haven't called me back?" It was BJ.

"BJ, what do you want?" I said being short with him.

"I want to see you," he said. I could hear the desperation in his voice.

"What's wrong?"

"I just need to see you. Can you come over?" he said.

Every fiber in my body was telling me no, that I shouldn't go over there, but I just couldn't say no. "I'll be there in a minute," I said regretting the words as soon as they came out of my mouth.

I excused myself from the cute New Yorker and headed for the front door. As I made my way through the crowd, I felt someone grab my arm.

"Where do you think you're going?" It was Eric.

"Oh, Eric, sorry, but I have to do something."

"You're on your way to see that boy," he said. Eric had a strange look on his face.

"Eric, let go of my arm, and it's none of your business where I'm going."

"Actually, it is my business." Eric replied.

This boy has completely lost his mind. I snatched my arm away from him. "Eric, pull yourself together," I said glaring at him as I stormed out the front door.

He followed behind me. "I wouldn't go over there if I were you!" he shouted at me.

"Eric, you're drunk! Go back in the house and leave me the hell alone!" I said as I jumped in my car and sped off.

Eric had completely lost it. How many times did I have to tell him I was not interested? I was fuming by the time I pulled up to BJ's apartment. Eric had really pissed me off. I got out of the car and stormed up to BJ's door. I noticed a car parked across the courtyard with its headlights on. When I got out of my car the headlights went out. *Probably just some kids,* I thought to myself as I knocked on BJ's door.

BJ answered the door after one knock. "Oh, baby, I missed you," he said pulling me close to him and kissing me on my neck.

I resisted, pushing him away.

"What's wrong, baby?"

"BJ, I can't do this," I said moving into the house yet out of his reach.

"What can't you do?"

"This, BJ! It's not working. You know someone has been threatening me! And I can't be sure it's related to you, but who else could it involve? I haven't been seeing anyone else."

BJ's face frowned up. The creases in his forehead bulged out, and he began pacing back and forth. "That little bitch," he mumbled as he pounded his fist into his hand.

"BJ, who you talking to and who are you calling a bitch?" I said moving past him ready to leave.

He looked at me, "No . . . no, baby, not you," he said running to me.

"BJ, I have to go. I just wanted you to know I cannot see you anymore."

"No, don't leave," BJ jumped in front of me.

"BJ, move!" I said trying to push my way past him. Of course, I couldn't. He was much stronger than I was.

"I said no!" BJ snapped. His face was distorted; he looked as if he was going to explode. I began to get nervous; I wasn't for sure what he was capable of.

"BJ, please move," I said.

He grabbed me by both arms. His grip was cutting off the circulation in my arm. "Not after all I've sacrificed! You think you're gonna just walk out my life!" He was yelling now—spit flying from his mouth as he pronounced each word. Sweat was starting to form on his forehead.

"BJ, what is wrong with you?" I insisted. I squirmed trying to get out of his grasp.

BJ pushed me up against the wall. "I said you are not leaving!" he shouted.

I didn't know what to do. I couldn't believe this was happening. I continued to squirm. What was going on? Was BJ insane? I took the only recourse I could think of . . . I kneed him in the balls.

The impact of my knee to his testicles sent him doubling over in pain. In a flash, I grabbed my keys and ran out the front door, leaving BJ lying there moaning and groaning in pain. As I ran to my car, I noticed the headlights from earlier. I heard a female voice call out, "You faggot!" The car revved up and sped passed me narrowly missing me. I jumped in my car and drove off.

What was going on tonight? First, Eric acting funny, then BJ, and now someone trying to run me down. I left BJ's apartment with a vow never to return.

When I got home, I was visibly upset. I had been crying all the way home. I just wanted to crawl into bed. To my surprise, Michael was still up.

"Hey, Tristan, how was your night?" Michael said. He was lounging on the couch watching an old black and white movie and chomping down some popcorn. Why couldn't my life be that simple? Michael enjoyed every minute of life. I wish I had just a piece of his happiness.

I tossed my keys on the counter. "I don't want to talk about it," I said heading for my room.

Michael jumped out his seat. "What's wrong?" he asked following me.

I really didn't want to tell Michael. I was in no mood for him to judge me.

"Why are your clothes all messed up?" he pressed. "Have you been crying?"

I didn't answer.

"You were with that boy!" Michael said. His face frowned up. "Man, I told you," he said condescendingly.

"Michael, I don't feel like a lecture. I already know what you gonna say," I stopped him.

"Well, since you know me so well, I won't say anything," he said as he turned and walked away.

I went into my room and shut the door. I wanted peace and quiet. Not five minutes had passed before Michael burst back into my room. He walked straight up to me. He was so close I could smell the popcorn on his breath. I could even hear his heart beating.

"Tristan, you don't know everything, and you don't know me like you think you do!" He was glaring at me.

"Well, why don't you tell me," I said.

"Tristan, you . . ." Michael trailed off. It was as if he wanted to tell me something but couldn't.

"What, Michael?"

Michael looked me in the eyes. It was like when Alicia looked at me. He was staring into my soul. My heart skipped a beat, and I backed away. Without saying a word, Michael turned around and walked away. *What was that about?* It was as if something was in the air making men act crazy. I fell asleep with a million unanswered questions.

CHAPTER 18

*L*abor Day weekend was a bust for me. After that first night turned out to be so horrible, I decided to stay home for the rest of the weekend. I pigged out on junk food and slept the entire time. Sunday, I helped a coworker work a wedding event, but other than that I stayed home. The week dragged on, in part because I was so looking forward to my mother's visit.

My mother decided she was going to stay in a hotel. Although I pleaded for her to stay at the house, she said she didn't want to be a burden. That was my mother. So I booked her a room at the Four Seasons downtown. I wanted her to enjoy her stay in Atlanta.

I did get some good news by Wednesday. Rashawn's doctor called and said I was a match, and I could donate my bone marrow as soon as possible. I called Kim to let her know.

"Oh, that's wonderful!" Kim shouted. I was at work when I called her. "Tristan, call Rashawn right now," she demanded. "We are going to have to celebrate."

"Well, it's not a guarantee, Kim," I said not wanting to get her hopes up. "I mean his body could reject my bone marrow."

"Well, at least it's worth a try," she said full of glee.

I got off the phone with her to call Rashawn. I was sure he already knew, but I needed to call him. I hesitated dialing his number. I wasn't sure what I was going to say. Kim had told me he was home recuperating from a grueling chemo treatment. I slowly dialed his number not quite sure how he would react on the other end. Rashawn picked up after a couple of rings.

"Hello," came his meek sounding voice. Rashawn just wasn't the same.

"Hey, Rashawn. This is Tristan," I said nervously.

"I know who it is," he said. He still had that smart mouth.

"Well, I'm sure you already know," I said.

"Yes, honey, I guess you want a gold medal or something," he responded.

No, he didn't! "Well, Rashawn, you don't have to be an ass about it," I said.

"Okay . . . okay, I'm sorry. Thank you, Tristan," he said. His voice had a sense of hope in it. I knew Rashawn had been praying for a miracle. I knew he had a tough outer shell, but deep down he prayed for God to save him. It was ironic that it was me who happened to be a match. I accepted Rashawn's apology because I knew it was going to be the closest I would get to him apologizing for what went down between us.

"Well, my momma will be here this weekend," I said changing the subject.

"Really? Miss Ruth coming to Atlanta? Shut up, girl! I didn't think she would ever step foot out of the city limits of Omaha," Rashawn said jokingly.

"Yeah, I can't wait," I said.

"You always were a momma's boy," Rashawn said before he began to cough violently.

"You okay, Rashawn?" I asked.

"I'm fine. You make sure you bring Miss Ruth by to see me," he said.

We said goodbye, and I smiled as I hung up the phone. I had gotten my friend back. I quickly called and made arrangements with the doctor. I wanted to donate my marrow while my mother was in town.

Thursday came and seemed to last forever. I constantly stared at the clock waiting for five o'clock to come. I busied myself with some last minute details for the event I was planning. Media attention surrounding Monty had died down, and it seemed everything was back on track. I was going over some swatches for the tables when I noticed the time . . . 5:15 p.m. Thank God. I gathered my things and headed out.

I had requested Friday off, so I could be at the airport to pick my mother up. I had decided to stay at the hotel with my mother. I felt Michael and I needed some space after the scene we had the other day. Besides I had booked a fancy suite, and I wanted to enjoy it with my mother. So I headed home to pack some clothes for the weekend.

Michael was working late, so I knew I didn't have to worry about bumping into him. As I headed to my car, my cell phone rang. The caller ID indicated it was BJ. He had been calling me all week leaving all sorts of messages saying he was sorry about what had happened. I decided to listen to my instinct and not answer his calls. I knew he would just suck me back into his life, and I didn't want that. So I ignored his call and headed home.

~~~

Finally, it was Friday morning. My mother's flight was due in at 11:45 a.m., so I slept in until nine. Michael had already left for work, so I showered and was out the door by ten. I wanted to stop by a flower shop and get some roses to greet my mom with. I reached the airport at 11:15 a.m., just in time to find a good parking spot. I waited at the top of the escalator where everyone else waited for their loved ones to ascend from the airport subway. Since 9/11, you weren't allowed in the terminal without a boarding pass.

I had explained how large Atlanta's airport was to my mother. I hoped she would be okay. I was holding twelve dozen red roses, my mother's favorite, and leaning against the wall with a bright smile on my face. The airport was crowded as usual. People were coming and going with both tearful goodbyes and cheerful hellos.

I checked my watch. It was 11:58 a.m. She should be showing up any minute. I looked around, getting a little impatient when I heard that sweet angelic voice.

"You never did have patience, my son," I turned around, and there was my mother. Just as perfect and beautiful as the last time I'd seen her. I don't know what came over me, but when we hugged, I just broke into tears. It felt good to be in my mother's arms. I felt safe.

"Baby, it's alright. Momma's here."

"Mom, where did you come from? I've been standing right here. I didn't see you come up the escalator?" I said through my tears.

"Oh, our flight got in early. We've been sitting in the food court for the past twenty minutes," she said.

"We?" I said, and just then Corey bounded around the corner.

"Surprise!" he shouted.

"Oh my God!" I said giving him a big bear hug. "I didn't know you were coming too," I said. My heart was overjoyed.

"I know. Momma wanted to surprise you," he said.

"It was hard to pry him away from that new baby," my mother added. "And are those for me?" she pointed towards the now crushed roses. I had been holding them in my hands while I hugged her and Corey.

"I'm sorry, Ma," I said handing her the tearstained, crushed flowers.

"It's okay, baby. I will still cherish them." She took the flowers, and we headed to go get their luggage.

"Trey, let's do the song," Corey said as we walked towards the baggage claim. My mother and I knew exactly what he was talking about.

"Corey, we're too old for that," I said.

"No, we ain't," he replied. Corey was a big kid at heart even though he was built like a linebacker. The song he was referring to was a rhyme we used to sing with our mother when we were kids.

"Okay," I said. Corey eagerly got on one side of my mother and me on the other. We linked arms and began to chant as we walked . . . .

> *"Anybody, anybody in our way*
> *If you don't get out our way*
> *We'll kick you out the way"*

We laughed and chanted the song over and over as if we were the only ones in the airport. It was as if we were kids all over again. It felt good.

CHAPTER 19

*C*orey talked a mile a minute. He was so excited about being in a big city. "Man, we have to go out tonight. I want to see some fine honeys," he said. We had checked into the hotel and were unpacking. The room was a grand two bedroom suite. There was a living area and even a small kitchen. It was nicer than most apartments I had visited. The ceilings were high, and the windows were large. We had a perfect view of downtown from the fourteenth floor. My mother took one room, and Corey and I took the other.

"Did I show you the baby pictures?" Corey asked. Our mother had sent me some in the mail, but I let Corey show me again.

"He's beautiful, Corey," I said.

"Yeah, man, don't he look like me?" Corey said with the smile of a proud poppa plastered on his face.

Actually, he didn't look like anyone. He was such a newborn that you couldn't make out who he was going to look like, but I went along with Corey. "Yeah, he does look like you," I said patting Corey on the back.

"Corey, put those pictures away," mom said from the other room. "Now we didn't come all this way to sit in a hotel room. Let's go!" My mother hated wasting time.

"What are we going to do?" Corey asked once we were back in the car.

"Well, first I thought we would look at a couple of apartments. I mean that is what Momma came for, so we might as well get that over with," I said.

"Sounds good to me," my mother said.

"Okay," Corey said, "but then can we go to Lenox Square Mall? My boy back home said that's where all the stars be?" Corey added.

"Sure," I said as I made my way through traffic.

We looked at several different apartments, all in different parts of town. They were either too expensive, too small, or in one instance, too dangerous. It was getting late in the afternoon and traffic was getting heavy.

"Let's make one more stop," I said. My mother and brother looked worn out. We were in an area not too far from Lenox Square, so I figured we could stop before we went to the mall. I pulled up to The Beaumont Apartment Homes.

"These look nice," my mother said as she got out the car. The apartments were very nice. The surrounding land was a sprawling, well-manicured lawn. There was a little cottage with a sign that indicated the leasing office. Immediately, I thought this was out of my price range.

"I don't know, Ma. This looks too expensive," I said.

"Come on. We're already here, so we might as well give it a try," my mother said. We were greeted by an attractive, young, black woman probably in her late twenties.

"Welcome to The Beaumont!" she said. Corey immediately perked up. "How can I help you guys?" she asked smiling at Corey. He always caught women's attention.

"Well, I'm looking for a one bedroom apartment," I said.

"Have a seat," she offered. I introduced myself, my mother, and my brother.

"How bout you, sir? Do you need an apartment as well?" she asked Corey in a flirtatious manner.

"No, shawty, I'm just here visiting my big bro," he said.

My mother popped Corey on the hand putting him in check. He had a baby momma waiting on him at home, and Miss Ruth didn't play that. I giggled to myself watching my brother get chastised.

"We have a couple of styles of one bedrooms, ranging from $600 to $800 a month," said Mary, the leasing agent.

Wow, $600 a month was a good price, especially for this area. She took us on a tour of the property; there was a fitness center, swimming pool, and computer lab. The apartment we looked at was perfect for me. It had one bedroom and one bath, not too big and not to small. There was a huge bay window that overlooked a courtyard. It was perfect.

"Tristan, I like this," my mother said giving her approval, and at $600 a month, I liked it too.

Mary gave me some paperwork to fill out, and I agreed to return it with my application fee the following week. I had found an apartment in one day. Wow, I couldn't believe it!

After the apartment search, we headed to Lenox Square Mall for some lunch and shopping. My phone rang while we were eating. I ignored the call when I realized it was BJ.

"Why you didn't answer that?" Corey asked as he chomped on his burger.

"Because I didn't want to talk," I said.

After lunch, we began shopping. My mother brought a baby tee that said "I Love My Grandma" for her new grandson and a little, pink dress for her granddaughter. She also splurged on a Coach purse for herself. Corey brought himself some new tennis shoes.

"Man, we don't even have these Jordan's in the O. My boys are going to be so mad," he said.

Right before we were leaving, Corey spotted Jermaine Dupree in Nordstrom. "Oh my God!" Corey shouted as he ran up to an unsuspecting Jermaine. "Man, I got all your records. You're tight as hell!" Corey said. Jermaine was polite and shook Corey's hand before signing a piece of paper Corey pulled out his pocket.

As we headed back to the hotel, I felt so complete. My family was together although they were pooped. Corey was half asleep in the back seat, and my mother was dozing off in the front passenger seat.

BJ called again, and I ignored his call. "Sweetie, who is that you keep ignoring?" my mother asked. I thought she was sleep also.

"No one, mom," I said.

We pulled up to the hotel and headed to the room for a nap. I had arranged for a spa treatment for my mother that evening, which was also a great way to give my brother and me a chance to hang out.

"So what church do you go to, son?" my mother asked as we lounged across her bed. It was a big king size bed with lots of blankets and pillows. It was big enough for all three of us. Corey had already fallen asleep. The plane ride and apartment search were a bit much for him. My mother and I sat up talking.

I told her about my church, New Beginnings, and the Sunday Brunch Club, what was left of it anyway. "We don't have Sunday brunch as often," I admitted, "but I try to go to church as often as possible."

"Well, that sounds nice, Tristan. I would love to meet your friends. Maybe we can go to church this Sunday, and I'll cook for you guys?" she offered.

"Oh, that would be great, Ma," I said.

My phone rang again. Of course it was BJ. I ignored it. My mother gave me that "I know something's up" look.

"Who do you keep dodging, Tristan?" she asked while stroking my hair. I didn't want to tell her, but I knew she would press. I told her all about BJ and the threatening letters. She looked at me then pulled me close.

"Son, sometimes it's best to face the truth rather than run away from it," she said. "You need to make sure you pray and keep God first. He'll never steer you wrong," she added. As I contemplated the words of advice my mother gave me, I fell asleep. Soon all three of us were in dreamland together.

Later that evening, my mother had her spa treatment, and Corey and I headed out for a little brother to brother time. We ended up at Club 112 later that night. Corey seemed to have a good time. He flirted with all the ladies while I sat in a corner sipping a drink. After the club, we headed back to the hotel, but first I needed to stop by the apartment. I'd left some papers for work that I wanted to go over.

"That club was tight," Corey said. "I've never seen that many fine honeys in one place."

"I'm glad you had fun," I said. It was a great club; I had never been, so it was nice to try something new.

I pulled up to the high-rise. "This is where you live?" Corey asked. "Man, what does your boy do for a living?" he said referring to Michael.

"You can come in, but you have to be quiet," I said. "Michael is probably asleep."

As we got out the car, I heard someone call my name. "Tristan!" At first I thought it was Corey. Then I realized Corey was standing right next to me.

"Who is that?" I said looking into the dark parking lot. A shadow emerged from the distance, and I could finally make out who it was . . . BJ. In an instant he was in front of us.

"So this is why you've been ignoring me?" BJ asked looking at Corey.

Corey immediately got on the defensive. "Yo, Trey, who is this cat?" Corey said stepping in front of me ready to knock BJ to the ground. Corey was smaller than BJ, but he certainly wasn't scared of him.

"BJ, what are you doing here?" I said as angry as ever. BJ tried to step around Corey, but Corey held his ground.

"Oh, so you got another nigga? That's what it is?" BJ asked.

"I told you I didn't want to see you again!" I said.

"Yo, Trey, you want me to bust this nigga?" Corey said balling up his fist. Oh, God, I didn't want them to fight.

"Tristan, are you okay?" Rudolph, the night doorman, came outside. Thank God! Just in time.

BJ looked at Rudolph who had the phone in his hand ready to dial 911. BJ puffed his chest out at Corey, turned, and walked away. "I'm fine, Rudolph, thank you," I said as we walked inside. "This is my brother, Corey," I said introducing them.

We made our way up the elevator. "Man, who was that, Trey? I was ready to bust that nigga straight in the jaw," Corey said. It sounded like he'd had one too many drinks.

"He's no one, Corey. Just someone who doesn't know how to take no for an answer," I said as we made our way to Michael's apartment. I took out my key and opened the door. Corey was stunned again.

"This crib is tight as hell," Corey said as we walked in.

"Shhh!" I said, "I told you my roommate is sleeping."

"No, I'm not," Michael said scaring the crap out of me.

"Oh, Michael, I didn't think you would be up," I said. I introduced Michael and Corey.

"I didn't know your brother was going to be here?" Michael said. "You should have told me. I would've gone out too."

"Your place is tight, man. I like this a lot," Corey said. I left the two of them in the living room talking while I ran to my room to get what I'd came for.

"Tristan, what's this about some guy following you to the apartment?" Michael said as I walked back into the living room.

"Corey, you have a big mouth," I said.

"I was 'bout to knock that nigga out. He just walked up on us like he was 'bout to do something," Corey continued.

"Shut up, Corey!" I said.

"I'm not going to say anything," Michael said shaking his head.

"Don't worry, Michael. I found an apartment, so I should be ready to move soon." I knew Michael was ready for me to go.

"Oh," Michael said getting quiet.

"Well, we have to go. I'm staying at the hotel with Corey and my mom this weekend."

"Well, I would like to meet your mother?" Michael said.

"You will on Sunday. She's cooking over here if you don't mind." I said. I'd meant to ask Michael about that earlier, but I figured he wouldn't mind.

"Oh, really?" Michael said.

"Yeah, and we're all going to church," I said as Corey and I walked out the door.

"Well, I'll be sure to be there," Michael said shutting the door behind us.

CHAPTER 20

Michael

"So Tristan has found an apartment," Michael said to himself as he shut the door behind Corey and Tristan. You would think that Michael would be happy, but he wasn't. He was certainly confused, however. Michael went to the fridge, grabbed a soda, and made his way to the couch. He hadn't been sleeping much with everything that was on his mind. He knew one day he was going to have to face the truth, and it seemed that day was coming oh too quickly. Michael had a secret. He had kept the secret since college. Only one person knew what Michael was hiding, and that was Tracy.

Tracy and Michael became friends their freshman year in college. They were both very attractive people, so it was natural that they would start dating. They dated for all of freshman year. Tracy never thought anything of the fact that they never had sex . . . mainly because she was still a virgin and wasn't ready to have sex. However, after a year passed and her sexual appetite began to kick in, it was to her amazement when Michael sat her down and said he wasn't sure if he even liked women at all. Michael wasn't sure, but he thought he might be gay. With the close relationship Michael had with Tracy, she was the only person he trusted to tell this to.

"Have you acted on this desire?" Tracy demanded to know between tears. She was heartbroken. Michael was the man she wanted to give her virginity to. Michael swore he had never been with another man and he would never cheat on her, but he knew his desires would soon get the best of him. Tracy believed him. Michael was too much of a good guy to cheat on her. So they became close friends.

Michael had struggled with his sexuality since then, but he'd never actually been with a man. In fact, he hadn't had sex with anyone since his declaration to Tracy that he may be gay. Of course there were a few failed attempts, but never had Michael went all the way with a man. Now all those feelings were back, and they were stronger than ever. Tristan had awakened all those feelings that Michael had kept bottled inside. Michael lay on the couch tormented. What was he going to do? Michael fell asleep on the couch with unanswered questions still looming over his head.

CHAPTER 21

Tristan

Saturday was just as wonderful as Friday. I took my mother to Kim's shop to get her hair done. Corey drooled over Kim the whole time we were there. "Kim, thank you so much," my mother said admiring her new do. My mother tried to pay Kim, but Kim refused to accept the money.

"Ms. Ruth, no, I can't accept that. How about repaying me by having me over on Sunday for some of that good cooking Tristan has told me about?" Kim said pushing my mother's money away.

"Of course, my sweetie," my mother said with glee. This made Corey's day as well. He couldn't wait until Sunday so he could flirt with Kim.

After we left the shop, we headed down to the famous Auburn Avenue to visit Dr. Martin Luther King's historical neighborhood and gravesite. My mother always wanted to visit the site, so she was very excited to finally be there. We took in as much of Atlanta as we possibly could in such a short amount of time. By the end of the day, we were pooped. Our final stop was the grocery store. My mother wanted to buy the food she was going to cook for Sunday dinner.

"Why don't we stay at the apartment?" I suggested. "That way you can get a head start on the cooking."

"Yeah, Ma! My man, Mike's apartment is nice," Corey added sounding like a kid in a candy store. I was sure Michael wouldn't mind especially considering he was going to get a home cooked meal.

"Where will we sleep?" my mother asked as we went through the line at the grocery store.

"You can take my bed, and Corey and I will camp out in the living room." It was settled. We finished up at the grocery store, stopped by the hotel to pack our clothes, and headed to the apartment.

Michael was home when we got there. "Nice to meet you, Ms. Smith," Michael said. He always had a suave, cool demeanor even when meeting someone's parents.

"Well, aren't you handsome," my mother said making Michael blush, which was hard to do considering he was black as night.

"Make yourself at home, Ms. Smith," he offered. Michael showed my mom to the kitchen and helped her put away the groceries while Corey and I sat in the living room talking.

It was good talking to Corey; he had a lot to catch me up on. He had gotten promoted at work, and he and his girlfriend were talking about marriage. We became so engrossed in our conversation that I didn't even realize how late it was.

"Michael, where is my mother?" I asked after I looked at the clock that read 11:30 p.m.

"She went to bed a while ago," he said. "And I think if y'all are going to church, you better go to bed as well," he added. Michael went into his room and returned with a load of blankets tossing one to Corey and one to me before returning to his room to go to bed. Corey and I made ourselves comfortable just like when we were kids making pallets in the living room.

"Trey?" Corey said as we lay in the dark.

"What's up?" I replied half asleep.

"Michael's a good guy. I like him," Corey said. "What's up with you two?" he added. The question kind of took me by surprise

"He's straight, Corey," I mumbled before drifting off to dreamland.

~~~

Sunday morning was perfect. The whole gang was together for church minus Eric. Tyler said Eric couldn't make it for some reason. He wasn't sure. But Kim, Michael, Tyler, and even Rashawn came out for Sunday service. My mother was very pleased to see Rashawn; she embraced him and gave him some of her motherly love.

Church was as good as ever. The bishop had the church all in a frenzy preaching about one's "due season." He even had Rashawn going to the altar during altar call. I think Rashawn was looking for a divine intervention. We were checking into the hospital Monday morning for the surgery. Rashawn was supposed to be in the hospital right then, but he refused. He wanted to be at church.

After church, we headed to the apartment for a feast of turkey, dressing, macaroni and cheese, greens, and my favorite, sweet potato pie. It was as if it was Thanksgiving. My mother had thrown down. We all had big bellies by the time we were done.

"Momma, you really out did yourself," I proclaimed as I sat back on the couch and unbuttoned the top button of my pants; I had eaten way too much. We all talked, laughed, and had a good time, all except Michael. He was distant for some reason. After he finished his food, he excused himself and went to his room. No one noticed, but I sure did.

"So, Tristan, are you ready to give up your bone marrow?" Rashawn said while we devoured slices of sweet potato pie.

"As ready as I'll ever be," I said. "The doctor said I'll be in and out. You're the one we're all worried about."

"Oh, don't worry 'bout me," he said.

"Rashawn, be serious," Kim said. "You need to take better care of yourself." Kim had a stern look on her face which meant she was serious.

"You know Kim's right," my mother said. "Your body is your temple, and you must cherish it as a gift from God." We all listened as my mother dropped some of her wisdom on us. It began to get late and soon Kim, Tyler, and Rashawn were gone.

My mother went back to my room. She was tired from all the cooking, and my brother went down to the fitness center to work off all the food we had just eaten. I was going to go with him, but my body was worn out, and I couldn't move a muscle. So I directed Corey to the fitness center on the first floor and retired to the couch. I was in the middle of an *I Love Lucy* marathon when Michael came out of his room. He went into the kitchen without saying two words to me. What was his problem? He was like night and day with me, and I was fed up.

"Michael, what is wrong with you?" I asked catching him before he returned to his bedroom. He stopped in his tracks. "I don't understand. Why are you acting so strange? If it's because of what happened the other night with BJ, don't worry. I'll be out soon, and you won't have to deal with my bullshit anymore," I said.

I was standing in his face now. He tried to move past me, but I wouldn't let him. "Come on, Michael. Say something. I thought we were better than this," I pressed. "You wanted me to move out, so that's what I'm doing."

"Tristan, I really don't want to talk about it," Michael replied.

"Why not, Michael? I thought we were friends," I said getting angry.

Michael stared at me in the eyes; they pierced through me sending chills down my back.

"Tristan, you're not ready for what I have to say," Michael said.

Emotions were flooding through my body. The tension was so thick between the two of us you could literally see it. "What do you mean? I'm tired of you acting like you have all the answers. Just say what's on your mind!"

Michael moved back from me giving himself room. "Maybe it's me that's not ready," he said looking down at the floor.

"Talk to me, Michael. Tell me what's wrong. Is it José? I know you've been grieving over the lost of that little boy," I said.

"No, that's not it," he said moving further away. "Tristan, it's hard for me. I don't know what to do sometimes. I mean sometimes I just wish you hadn't come into my life," he said. He was still looking at the ground.

What did he mean he wished I hadn't come into his life? Michel kept talking.

"Before you, it was all so simple. I just lived my life, and that was that. Then you came along," he said.

"What are you saying?" I asked.

Michael hesitated. Sweat was forming on his forehead. "Tristan . . . I think . . . I think I love . . . you."

WHAT! Were my ears deceiving me? Did he say what I think he said? Michael stood there in the kitchen looking down at the tile floor. I could tell that was the hardest thing in the world for him to say. There was silence for what seemed like an eternity. I really didn't know what to say, so I said the first thing that came to my mind.

"I thought you wanted me to move out?" As soon as I said that I felt stupid.

Michael finally looked up at me. "Tristan, I'm confused. I know that much, but I was so angry and a little jealous when I walked in your room and found BJ in your bed," he admitted.

"I . . . I thought you were straight," I said nervously.

"I don't know what I am, Tristan, but I know my feelings are real, and I don't want you to leave." Michael started to walk closer to me.

I couldn't believe it . . . could this be really happening? Any minute I was expecting for someone to pinch me and wake me from this beautiful, beautiful dream. But it wasn't a dream; I knew this because Corey walked in just then.

"Yo, Trey, that fitness room was off the hook. The honeys were all up in there. Too bad you don't like the ladies!" Corey was oblivious to the conversation Michael and I were having. Corey went into the kitchen and grabbed a bottle of water out the fridge before heading for the shower.

Michael and I were still standing in the same spot. Neither of us knew what to say. "It's late, Tristan, and you have a big day ahead of you. I'm going to let you go to bed," Michael finally said. He went into his room and shut the door leaving me still standing there in the kitchen bewildered.

CHAPTER 22

The surgery wasn't as bad as I thought it would be. I must admit I was a little nervous. My mother, Corey, and Michael went with me to the hospital. The doctor said I was going to receive a local anesthesia, and I would be released a few hours after the surgery. Yvette and a few others from the office had called that morning to give me well wishes. Yvette said what I was doing was very admirable. I didn't look at it like that; I was just helping a friend in need.

Since I would need a little time to recuperate, Yvette told me to just work from home for a while. As I lay in the hospital bed waiting for the doctor to come in to whisk me off to surgery, I thought about what had happened the night before. Michael hadn't said much to me since then.

"Tristan, I'm about to go get some coffee. I'll be right back," my mother said.

"I'm coming too, Momma." Corey jumped out his seat and tagged behind our mother. That left Michael and I alone in the room.

"Michael, are you okay?" I said trying to adjust myself in the hospital bed. Michael was staring out the window.

"Oh, I'm good. Just a little worried about you," he said.

I smiled. I had butterflies in my stomach. I wasn't sure if it was nerves from the pending surgery or the fact that Michael and I were alone for the first time. Michael turned and walked over to my bedside. "I have to go to work, Tristan, but I promise I'll be back by the time you wake up." He stroked my head and my heart began to pound. His touch was soft, yet firm. "I meant what I said last night, Tristan. I do love you . . ."

Michael trailed off, and then leaned in and kissed me on the lips. His tongue gently eased into my mouth, and he gave me the most passionate kiss I had ever felt. My body shivered. I was in a trance as Michael walked out the room. My mother and brother returned shortly after with the doctor in tow.

After he explained the procedure again, I was taken away to the operation room. My mom prayed out loud as they wheeled me down the hall. There wasn't much that I remembered about the surgery except that the nurse asked me to count to ten. The next thing I remember I was waking up back in my hospital room. Michael held true to his word. He was the first face I saw when I woke up. I adjusted my eyes as I tried to focus.

"Michael, you made it back," I said instantly smiling. The butterflies were returning to my stomach.

"Didn't I say I'd be back?" he said. A couple hours passed, and I was released to go home. The doctor explained that Rashawn was scheduled for surgery later that evening, and we were free to come visit him once he was in recovery. His surgery was more evasive, and he would be in recovery longer than I was.

I was feeling really fatigued, so Michael promised to come back to check on Rashawn for me. I spent the rest of the day lounging on the couch watching movies with my mother and brother. They were flying out in the morning, so I wanted to get in as much time with them as possible.

As I lay on the couch, stretched out with my head in my mother's lap, she stroked my hair. "Baby, I had a little talk with Michael," my mother said. My eyes got wide. "Tristan, I can see honesty in his eyes. I know he has struggled with dealing with his feelings, but I want you to have patience." I guess that was my mother's way of telling me she approved of Michael. This time I was going to listen to my heart.

The next morning I cried a bucket of tears when I took my family to the airport. "Don't cry, big bro. We'll see you soon," Corey said giving me a big bear hug. I held on tight like it was the last hug I would ever get from him. He smiled and punched me in the arm before saying goodbye.

My mother kissed me on the forehead and whispered in my ear, "Just remember to let go and let God."

I watched them leave and cried as I drove back to the apartment. I had tons of work to do for the event I was planning, so I engulfed myself in my work to keep from thinking about my mother and brother. My phone rang while I was working. It was Kim.

"Hey, Kim!" I said glad for the distraction.

"Hey, Trey, how are you feeling?"

"Good. I'm going to go back to work tomorrow."

"Well, Rashawn is doing better," Kim said. "He's still in the hospital, but the transplant went well. Thank you so much, Tristan."

"It was nothing, Kim. Hey, how are you? I know you have a lot going on."

"Well, it's been hard, but I'm good. You know Kevin has been living with me. Although Jamal loves having his daddy around, he's been driving me crazy, especially since he has gotten all holy. He's tripping, saying my clothes are too revealing. I have to keep telling him he is not my man. Oh, and then Brandon started calling me all of a sudden. I guess his other woman got tired of him."

That last comment shocked me. "What?" I said. "How do you know he has another woman?"

"Come on! Why else would he just stop calling me out of the blue, especially when everything was going so well between us?" Kim had a point. "I know something isn't right with Brandon. I just haven't put my finger on it," she added.

"Well, I have some news," I said smiling to myself.

"What is it, Trey?"

I told Kim all about Michael's declaration of love.

"Oh my God, Tristan! This is big! You bitch! I hate you!" she joked, and we laughed. "So now what?" she asked.

"We are going out on a date this weekend, and then we'll play it by ear."

"So I guess you're not moving out now," Kim said. She guessed right. In fact, I had torn up the application I had gotten from the apartment complex. I just prayed I wasn't getting ahead of myself. "I'm so happy for you, Tristan," Kim said.

"Say, have you been getting any more of those letters?" Kim asked.

"Actually, no. Since that last one, I haven't received anymore. Maybe it was just someone playing a joke," I said.

"Well, even so, be careful. I have to go. Kevin's physical therapist just arrived. I love you, Trey, and I'll check in with you later." We hung up, and I returned to my work.

CHAPTER 23

Eric

Eric's sister was becoming irrational. She was constantly calling on Eric to calm her down, threatening to put an end to Brandon's life. Eric decided to cool it with the letters he had been sending Tristan, especially since his mother was in town. Besides, it wasn't fun watching Tristan squirm anymore, and he needed to devote his time to Lisa. She seemed so fragile.

One morning when he was supposed to meet up with the gang at church, Lisa called crying saying she was in severe pain. So instead of church, Eric ended up in the emergency room with Lisa. The doctor said Lisa was experiencing premature labor, probably due to stress. She was placed on medication to stop the labor and instructed to remain on bed rest.

"Lisa, you have got to get a hold of yourself," Eric said as they sat waiting for the doctor.

"I know Eric; I don't know what's wrong with me. I'm so angry all the time; you know I busted the windows out of Brandon's car after I followed him one night. He went over to Tristan's house."

Oh no, Eric thought, *now Lisa knows where Tristan lives.* "Well, Lisa, if you don't stop, you're going to harm the baby," he said.

Lisa was looking horrible lately. Of course her weight was picking up, and it looked as if her hair was falling out. Eric was truly worried for his sister's health.

"I think Tristan knows Brandon is married," Lisa said.

"How do you know?" Eric asked.

"Well, when I followed Brandon to Tristan's place, they got into a heated argument, and Tristan told Brandon to stay out of his life. And one day when I was sitting outside of Brandon's apartment, Tristan ran out with an angry look on his face."

Eric was taking all this in. Of course this was good news to him. "Listen, Lisa, I want you to focus on your health and the baby. Leave Brandon and Tristan alone!" Eric pleaded with Lisa.

"Whatever, Eric," she responded.

Eric took Lisa home, placed her in bed, and watched as she fell asleep. Eric felt sorry for Lisa. She was lonely, depressed, and carrying the child of a cheater. As she slept, Eric thought of ways to get back at Brandon for being a horrible excuse of a man.

CHAPTER 24

Tristan

M y first date with Michael was marvelous although I was nervous as ever. The date started early Saturday morning. I awoke to a big breakfast that Michael had prepared. As I ate, he stood in the kitchen with a big grin on his face watching me.

After breakfast we drove out to Stone Mountain. Michael wanted to take me hiking. Although I wasn't exactly an outdoorsman, I decided to give it a try. Michael said it was his favorite thing to do. This explained his solid thighs and firm, tight butt, which I admired from behind as I dragged along.

After the hike, we had lunch at the top of the mountain. It was nice. Michael had packed sandwiches, fruit, and even a little wine. As we ate, we talked to each other as if it was our first time meeting. Michael told me about his struggle with his sexuality and being forced to face the truth when he was dating Tracy. I asked him when he knew he loved me.

"Tristan, I loved you from the first time we saw each other at work," he responded. My heart skipped a beat.

I told him about my life, about how I was scared of dying alone, and how I yearned for kids. "Tristan, I would never leave you, and we could have as many kids as you wanted," he said. As we talked he stared so deep into my eyes. It was as if we were connected in a way so deep that it couldn't be broken.

After lunch we made our way down the mountain. Halfway down, I jumped on Michael's back and let him carry me. Of course we got a few stares, but we didn't care. We were having the time of our lives.

We decided to stop by Heaven's House to visit the kids. Alicia was in such a playful mood that when we left, Michael and I both had smiles on our face. The date wasn't over either. It was starting to get late in the evening, so we headed home to shower and change before going to Copeland's for dinner and drinks.

By the end of the night, we were worn out and a little tipsy. My sexual appetite was screaming out. I lusted for Michael. As we drove home my tool between my legs got harder and harder thinking about what we were going to do.

Once in the house, we began kissing uncontrollably. He tasted so good, and we were all over each other . . . then . . . "Wait . . . wait, Tristan," Michael said between kisses.

I didn't want to stop. I wanted to rip his clothes off. "What, Michael?"

"I don't want to do it like this. I want it to be perfect," he said. He sat me down on the couch and cupped my face with his hands looking me directly in the eyes. "Tristan, I've waited this long, and I just want this moment to be right. I want us to really know each other. I want you to love me as much as I love you," he said.

I was disappointed, but he had a point. Meaningless sex has gotten me in enough trouble as it was, so why not do it the right way this time. Michael escorted me to my room, undressed me, and placed me in the bed. Once I was tucked in, he gave me a passionate kiss before leaving. "Good night, Tristan," he said in a seductive tone. The liquor had really kicked in, so I was asleep in no time; that night, I experienced the best sleep of my entire life.

Over the next few weeks, Michael and I dated and got to really know each other. At night we would snuggle on the couch and watch movies or read. Every night he would tuck me in my bed before retiring to his room. It had been three weeks, and we hadn't had sex yet.

One day I was working late. It was getting close to the Exodus party, and I was working overtime. The office was empty when I headed home at eight o'clock. Michael had left work several hours earlier, and I was looking forward to going home and relaxing with him in front of the T.V. I drove home as quickly as possible. Michael was so sweet to me. He made me feel special; I realized I loved him too. I was seriously, deeply in love. I was excited to get home and be in his arms.

Once I was home, I opened the door. Everything was pitch black. Michael must not have been home after all. I was a little disappointed because I wanted to see him. I headed to my room and noticed light coming from under my door. I knew I didn't leave my light on. I opened the door and my heart jumped.

There were candles lit all over my room and rose petals spread across my bed. Two glasses of wine were on my night table, and the room smelled of soft lilac from the candles I presumed. I couldn't believe it. Michael was so perfect.

"Surprise," Michael's deep, chocolate voice whispered in my ear from behind. I turned around to find Michael standing there completely naked. What a sight it was! His skin was an even, dark skin, smooth all over. Not an ounce of hair was on his well-toned body. His stomach was so flat you could eat Thanksgiving dinner off it, and his tool was long and strong. I sighed. I was in heaven, or my version anyway.

Michael pushed me into the room and began kissing me all over. His kisses left a trail of wetness down my neck and my back as he pulled my shirt off. Without saying a word, he began to massage my body making me feel relaxed and loose. Soon my pants were off, and we were in the bed.

I kissed Michael back. I kissed his neck and his chest. I even kissed his arm. I wanted to taste every inch of him. As we became entangled in the sheets, our bodies became one. Our love making was soft and smooth, the best feeling I had ever experienced. We both moaned and groaned in ecstasy. The sounds oozed from our mouths and slipped into the night air.

Soon I was reaching a new high. I climaxed with Michael pushing inside of me. I gripped his back and let out a moan as he did the same. We lay there, our sex funky and loving every minute of it. Before I fell asleep, I whispered, "I love you, Michael."

He said, "I know you do . . . I love you too."

We fell asleep in each other's arms. Life was finally perfect. Or so it seemed.

CHAPTER 25

Brandon

*B*randon had no other recourse but to return home to his wife. Lisa was putting herself and their unborn baby in danger. She was turning into a mad woman, and since Tristan didn't want to have anything to do with him, he felt he might as well go home. He even tried a last minute attempt to hook up with Kim, but she quickly shot him down. It was the last straw when Lisa got rushed to the hospital. He knew then he had to go home.

Although Lisa was fed up with Brandon, she welcomed him with open arms. It was a minor victory for her. She had gotten her man back, for now. All was right with the world. She didn't even need to lean on Eric as much although she was so grateful to her little brother. She felt she wouldn't have made it this far without him.

As Brandon and Lisa began to nurse old wounds, Brandon even considered going to a marriage counselor with Lisa. He still loved her, and he wanted to provide a home for his unborn child. The thoughts of having a baby actually set well with him. It calmed him and even quieted his sexual appetite.

He still lusted for Tristan from time to time, and he was constantly tormented by the desires in his heart, but he dealt with it day by day. Several months had passed, and he hadn't thought about Tristan. Although Brandon and Lisa still had problems, they were making the best of it. Brandon was so busy trying to make his family work, he didn't even realize it was almost Thanksgiving. Atlanta had taken on a new look. The autumn leaves had fallen to the ground, and there was a refreshing crisp in the air. Brandon was feeling good about himself . . . . until one day.

Lisa decided they needed to go out for dinner. She was tired of sitting in the house. Her belly had begun to protrude, and she was getting morning sickness on a daily basis. Her doctor had taken her off bed rest, and with her stress level now down to a minimum, her hair began to grow back. So she decided they should go out for a night on the town.

They opted for dinner at Ruth's Chris Steak House an upscale restaurant. Brandon didn't exactly feel like spending a $100 on a meal they could have at home, but he didn't want to cause an argument, so Ruth's Chris it was. The restaurant was unusually noisy that night, and the hostess took her time seating them. She seemed to be preoccupied with something else. Lisa being the person she was of course recognized this and said something.

"Is there a problem, Miss?" Lisa asked obviously irritated.

"Oh, no ma'am. I'm sorry, but you know the singing group Exodus? Well, they are here tonight," the hostess exclaimed with glee.

"You mean that group with the faggot in it?" Lisa said rolling her eyes and rubbing her belly.

The hostess gave Lisa a funny look and seated them in a corner near the front. Brandon noticed the table where the singing group was sitting. There was a crowd of people around the table and seated right next to one of the group members was Tristan!

Brandon's heart stopped. He hadn't seen Tristan in months, and now that he was looking at him all his feelings came rushing back like a tidal wave. The dark-skinned brother who was sitting awfully close to Tristan and had his arm around his waist didn't help either. Brandon was on fire. He couldn't even see straight. He wanted to run over there and snatch Tristan up. Of course he couldn't stay at the restaurant.

"Lisa, we have to go!" he demanded.

"Why? We just got here," she said.

"Yeah, but I don't want to eat here. Let's go somewhere else," he pleaded.

"No, Brandon, I'm hungry. We're staying here," she replied.

"Lisa, I said let's go!" Brandon demanded grabbing Lisa's arm and pulling her out her seat. The look in his eyes showed he meant business, so Lisa didn't fight back.

"Fine," Lisa said following behind Brandon. "I don't want to eat here with that faggot from that singing group anyways." Lisa was obviously referring to Monty, who still had pending charges against him for soliciting sex.

"Stop using that word," Brandon said.

"Why? Are you a faggot too?" she replied.

Brandon ignored her response as they hopped in the car and headed to another restaurant. The whole time Brandon thought about Tristan.

CHAPTER 26

Tristan

Time flies when you're happy. It was already the end of November. Michael and I had been having such a good time together that summer and fall kind of blended together as one. We were so happy and so in love. Each day we learned something new about each other, like how Michael grinds his teeth in his sleep. This was something I had to get used to since I'd moved into his room. My room was converted back into the guest room.

Michael and I did everything together which left little time for my friends. Kim would call, however, and give me updates on everyone. She told me how Rashawn was back at work and doing well in remission. Kevin was heavily into church, and they had started dating again. Kim felt she might as well give her baby's father another chance especially with the new turn in life he had taken. Besides, she realized how much she still loved him. Kevin had fully recovered from the accident and had found Jesus. His next step, according to Kim, was to find a job! Tyler had gotten a promotion at work, so he was always busy, and no one had really heard from Eric lately. Just as well. He was acting really creepy lately. I was so caught up with being in love and my work that I had barely even spoken with my mother. Although now that she was computer savvy, we e-mailed each other on a regular basis.

This particular day, I was having dinner with the group Exodus at Ruth's Chris Steak House. Michael came along as well as Yvette. We were celebrating the fact that the party was now in full bloom. Everything was done except a few minor details, and it looked to be a big star-studded event. As we sat at our table waiting on our order of drinks, a crowd began to form around our table. Young girls and even boys were trying to get pictures and autographs from the group. At one point I could have sworn I saw BJ, but I wasn't sure. And when I looked back, there was no one there.

"Here's to Winter's Paradise," Yvette said holding her glass in the air for a toast. We all toasted and drank. "You know I took a gamble on you, Tristan, but you pulled through," Yvette said. Her compliments were few and far between, so I took that in and savored the moment.

"I can't wait till the party, Tristan," Christy said. "You know we're getting ready to drop another album," she added.

"Yeah, man, it's good too!" Efrim added.

Monty didn't say much. He was back to his usually quiet self. But as we were leaving, Monty pulled me to the side. "What's up?" I asked as I adjusted my pants. I had eaten a little too much.

"Ummm, Tristan," Monty stammered. Monty had a strange look on his face like he was nervous. I was a little impatient because Michael was waiting on me. "Tristan, were you scared when you came out of the closet?" Monty asked revealing the truth about his sexuality. He stood before me completely vulnerable.

I felt pleased that Monty felt secure enough to confide in me. I patted Monty on the shoulder, "Everyone gets scared, but you have to have the courage to face your fear, Monty. You have my number.

Call me and we can talk. I'm here for you," I said. *I hope I was able to put Monty at ease*, I thought to myself as I ran to the car to join Michael.

"What was that about?" Michael asked.

"I think Monty is going to come out the closet," I replied.

"Good for him," Michael said as he leaned over and kissed my lips before putting the car in drive. Boy, I loved that man.

CHAPTER 27

Thanksgiving came and went way too quickly. Michael came home with me to Nebraska. My mother cooked a huge meal, and I got to meet my new nephew for the first time. At just about four months, he was finally starting to look like my brother. I couldn't get enough of him. "Man, you're gonna spoil my son," Corey said several times over the course of the weekend. I didn't care because I felt this close bond between me and little Corey Jr.

When Michael and I got back to Atlanta, we went to Heaven's House to visit Alicia and the other kids. Alicia was doing very well as far as her health was concerned, so we were able to take her to the park and the movies. I loved little Alicia. She gave me so much hope. I even thought about adopting her. When we dropped her off, she gave me a big hug and said, "I love you, Tristan." Then something strange happened. She said, "God is watching," before she bounded up the stairs to her room. What did she mean by that?

I had a long week ahead of me. There were exactly seven days until the Exodus party. I was so busy all week I barely had time to think. I had to coordinate flower arrangements and set designs. There was the media to deal with and the celebrity guest list that was growing by the day. Michael helped out when he could, but he was working hard on a project himself. We barely were able to ride to and from work together because of our crazy hours.

I decided to put my friends on the guest list. I thought it would be good to get everyone together. I called Kim up one night from the office to let her know. "That sounds like fun, Trey," Kim said after I gave her the news. "We can celebrate the fact that Rashawn is in remission."

"Oh yeah! Good idea, Kim. So this Saturday I'll have your names on the list," I said. "Be sure to tell Tyler and Eric," I added.

"Can we bring dates?" Kim asked. She was pushing it, but I knew she wanted to bring Kevin along.

"Sure, Kim. Let Rashawn, Eric, and Tyler know they can bring a guest as well," I said as I quickly updated my guest list. I needed to have it turned in to the head of security by the end of business on Thursday.

"Well, I'll see you then," Kim said before hanging up.

I wrapped up what I was doing and headed out the door. It was late and the parking lot was dark. I rushed to get to my car. Just as I was reaching for the door handle, I felt someone grab my shoulder. "Tristan!" The familiar booming voice came at me. I quickly turned around to find BJ standing in front of me.

It's funny what love can do for you. The lust I had for BJ was completely gone. He wasn't even remotely attractive to me anymore. "BJ, what the hell are you doing? Have you been following me?" I was angry, and this man had lost his mind.

"I just want to talk to you," he said moving close to me.

I got my mace ready; I had started carrying it around after BJ came to my apartment uninvited. "BJ, we have nothing to talk about. Go home to your wife!" I wasn't sure, but I figured he was married.

BJ's face turned white. "Tristan, I love you," he said still invading my space.

"BJ, please . . . don't do this," I replied. I opened my car door. "Leave me alone!" I yelled.

"Brandon, get your ass over here!" I heard a female voice call from the distance just as I was getting into my car. I couldn't make out who it was, but I saw the headlights of a car parked not far away. BJ turned around in shock as I put my car in gear and sped off. I made a mental note to get a restraining order against BJ as soon as I had some free time. I zoomed through the parking lot, leaving BJ and presumably his wife in the dust.

CHAPTER 28

Lisa

Lisa was fed up with Brandon. After the dinner incident, she knew something was up with Brandon, so she began following him again. To her dismay, she found him with Tristan again. She refused to let that faggot take her husband. She would rather lose him to another woman than to Tristan. So she called Eric to see what she should do.

Eric told her about the party Tristan was throwing for the group Exodus. Eric said he was allowed one guest and suggested she come along. She could confront him there. Lisa thought this was a good idea, but she had other plans as well. With her mind working in overdrive, Lisa knew she would have to resort to desperate measures.

CHAPTER 29

Brandon

How dare that bitch follow me! Brandon thought to himself. He was sick of Lisa, and he refused to pretend any longer. He also couldn't believe how Tristan could just turn on him that way. The more he thought about Tristan, the angrier he became. How dare he dismiss him after Brandon had poured his heart out to him? Brandon decided to pay Tristan a visit.

He heard on the radio about a party that was going down at Level 3. It was for the singing group Exodus. After Brandon saw Tristan with them at Ruth's Chris Steak House, he knew Tristan would be at the party. Since Tristan wouldn't talk to him, he figured he would just have to confront him there. As Brandon plotted what he would do, he thought to himself, *it's payback time*.

CHAPTER 30

Winter's Paradise

Saturday came quickly. It was the morning of December tenth, and the sun was shining brightly down on the world. It was as if God himself had painted a picture of a perfect day. Tristan woke up early to prepare for the long day he had before him. After a nice breakfast with Michael, he headed out to start the day. First stop was Level 3 to check on the set design. Then he had an appointment at the barber shop, and he needed to pick up his suit from the tailors. Tristan had awaken that morning with butterflies in his stomach, and they stayed with him the whole day. He was nervous for so many reasons if only he knew what the day had in store for him.

Kim and Kevin did there usual morning ritual. They had breakfast with Jamal and said their morning prayer. Kevin was excited about the celebrity party, and although Kim didn't show it, she was too. She had picked out a fly little number to wear to the party. Her hair was whipped, and she was ready to kick it.

Rashawn was happy to be feeling better. For the first time in a long while, he finally felt peace in his life. He was excited to party with the celebs and show them how it was done.

Eric woke up with a chip on his shoulder. He was so unhappy with his life and so jealous of Tristan at the same time. He looked forward to putting Tristan on the spot. For him, this was going to be fun.

Lisa woke up determined. She was determined to keep her husband, and she was also determined to get rid of Tristan once and for all. That is why the night before she'd purchased a gun from a shady dealer at a pawn shop. She wasn't sure what she was going to do with the gun, but she knew she was going to take back control of her family.

Brandon was tired of living life unhappy; he also was determined to take control of his life. So that morning he awoke with a plan. The gun that was under the seat of his car was going to be put to good use today.

By nine that night, the red carpet was laid, and the party was in full swing. The event was opened to the public at $50 a person and only the first two-hundred people would get in, so BJ made sure he was there early. He had no idea his wife was on her way there with Eric. He did, however, know he wouldn't be able to just walk in with a gun, so he made his way to the back of the club where he saw a crew carrying in tubs of ice.

Brandon's heart began pumping fast as he approached the men unloading the heavy tubs of ice. He thought quickly on his feet. None of the men seemed to be paying Brandon any attention, so he simply blended in with them and eased his way in through the back. It was easier than he thought, and it actually gave him a rush. Brandon felt like he was in a James Bond movie or something.

Once inside he spotted Tristan running around with a headset on shouting orders. He was dressed in an all white suit, and he looked great. Brandon quickly found a spot in a corner before Tristan had a chance to see him and planted himself there to wait for the perfect time.

Kim, Kevin, and Tyler arrived together. They were so thrilled you could literally see the excitement on their face. They walked the red carpet like they were celebrities. "Can you believe this?" Kim said to Tyler as they made their way up the red carpet.

"No, honey, I can't, and I feel so underdressed," Tyler said referring to the baggy jeans and oversized Sean John shirt he was wearing. There were all sorts of celebrities arriving. Kim pointed out a few: Usher, Kim Kardashian, even Bobby Brown.

Rashawn arrived shortly after. He walked the red carpet with ease like he had been doing it for years. Peachtree Street in front of the club had been shut down, so paparazzi were everywhere flashing pictures of stars and some regular people if they were fashionable. Of course, Rashawn got a few pictures shot of him. With his navy blue Prada suit, matching Prada shoes, and oversized Dolce and Gabbana glasses, he looked like an A-list star. His hair had started to grow back, so he had a little baby afro that he had twisted up like John Legend. He was gorgeous. Once inside he quickly found Kim and Tyler.

"Gurl, Tristan doing the damn thang!" Rashawn said twirling around as he walked up to the gang.

"Yeah, it does look good in here," Kim said as she gave Rashawn a hug. The club was decorated in all white. White drapes hung from the ceiling at all angles. There were ice sculptures and water fountains, and the tables were set up with ivory colored table cloths and beautiful centerpieces filled with white orchids. There was a display of jewelry, and the sign above it read "Winter's Paradise . . . with Tiffany & Co."

Frank Ski was the DJ, and he was playing all the latest music. He announced Exodus would be performing in a few moments. There was a table with a champagne tower; glasses of Moët were spilling over. Kim and Tyler grabbed glasses, Rashawn opted not to drink because of the medication he was on, and Kevin was acting all holier than thou so he refused liquor as well.

"More for us," Tyler said holding his glass in the air.

The music was good, and Kim and Tyler were having a great time. After about thirty minutes, Tristan and Michael joined them. "Hey, guys! I'm glad you could come," Tristan said.

"Hey, Michael," Tyler said in a singsong voice smiling.

"Hey, guys," Michael said.

"Y'all ready to party?!?!" Frank Ski screamed into the mic. The crowd which had suddenly increased considerably got enthused. "Y'all ready for Exodus?!?!" Frank said. "Let's give it up for OneStop Events and Tristan Smith who put this event together!" Frank announced. Tristan began to blush. Everyone clapped for him. Usher even came up to speak.

"Yo, I remember you from the mall. What up?" he said giving Tristan a handshake.

Just then Frank Ski dropped a beat. "Y'all ready?" he said as a strong bass line kicked in and the lights dimmed. A spotlight shined on the stage and out busted Christy. The crowd went crazy. She looked flawless as she began to sing the hook from their new single. Then Monty joined her and the crowd got even louder and by the time Efrim was on the stage, the whole club rocked with excitement.

Lisa was nervous as she and Eric arrived at the club. She didn't realize so many people would be there. She was glad she dressed up. Her belly was protruding, so she had to buy a new dress. She hid her gun in her purse and prayed she wouldn't get searched by security.

They arrived just as commotion was breaking out in front of the club. It seemed the cops wanted to open Peachtree Street back up. As Lisa and Eric walked up the red carpet to the front door the security guy started talking into his earpiece. "Can't leave now. I got two people trying to get in . . . . handle it . . . handle it . . . okay . . . okay. Here I come." The security guy took one look at Lisa's big stomach and waved her in. He then quickly patted down Eric, checked their names off the guest list, and sent them in.

Wow, that was easy, Lisa thought to herself as the security officer ran off. Lisa relaxed, her nerves now disappearing. Inside the music was loud. Exodus was still performing. "Let's find that punk," Lisa said. Eric immediately became nervous; he was rethinking this whole confrontation thing.

Meanwhile Brandon had knocked back a couple of drinks and was a little drunk. It was time to find Tristan. He spotted him hugged up with the guy from the restaurant. They looked happy as they swayed to the music. Brandon walked straight up to them and tapped Tristan on the shoulder. Tristan turned around and his jaw dropped.

"Brandon!" Kim said as she noticed Brandon tapping Tristan. Then it made sense to her. The scent that she recognized from Tristan, that was Brandon's cologne. "Oh my God!" she blurted out and immediately became sick to her stomach.

Kim's outburst caught the attention of everyone standing around them.

"Brandon, what the fuck is going on?" Kim shouted.

"Kim, you know BJ?" Tristan asked.

"BJ? His name ain't no BJ! This is Brandon!!!" Kim was red in the face.

"Gurl, this some movie type shit!" Rashawn said looking on anxiously.

"Yo, what the hell? Who is this cat?" Kevin asked stepping in front of Kim. By now a little crowd had formed around the group. As Exodus sang away on stage, a mini drama was unfolding.

"BJ, what are you doing here?" Tristan demand. He was furious. "I'm calling the police!" The veins in Tristan's head were popping out indicating just how angry he was. BJ had turned into a stalker, not to mention he had been dating Kim as well.

Kim still had a look of horror on her face. She was pale and on the verge of vomiting. Brandon looked strange like he was about to do something. Michael noticed this and stepped in front of Tristan.

"Man, I'm going to have to ask you to leave," Michael said forcefully.

Brandon held his ground. "I'm not leaving here until I talk to Tristan," Brandon demanded.

"Please, BJ, just leave!" Tears started to stream down Tristan's face. The music was still pumping loudly, but the crowd had stopped paying attention to the music and was now focused on the drama.

Tristan realized he still had his headset on. "I need security to the main level front bar," he said into the mouthpiece.

Brandon reached out and grabbed Tristan. "I wouldn't do that," he said. Brandon was sweating profusely, and he had an evil glare in his eye.

"Get your hands off him," Michael demanded, and before anyone knew it, Brandon was on the ground. Michael had swung and landed a left hook right on Brandon's jaw. The impact was hard and could be heard over the loud music. It sent Brandon tumbling to the ground. Brandon quickly scrambled to his feet reached in his pocket and pulled out the .48 revolver. The shinny pistol glowed under the florescent club lights. Although what happened next only took a few seconds, it seemed like an eternity.

Michael noticed the gun first and pushed Tristan to the ground. Kim screamed at the top of her lungs which caused Kevin to react by lunging toward Brandon. Before Kevin reached him, Brandon pointed the gun at his own temple and uttered the words "Tristan, I loved you" before pulling the trigger. Blood and brain matter splattered everywhere as Brandon's now limp body fell to the floor. The music stopped and people began running for the door. Tristan, Michael, Rashawn, Kim, and Kevin stood there in shock at the dead body that lay in front of them.

"Oh my God!" a female voice said from behind them. Everyone turned to see Eric and a familiar lady standing behind them. The woman with Eric was obviously pregnant. "What have you done?" the pregnant woman shouted as she ran to Brandon's body lying on the ground in a puddle of blood. Tristan recognized the woman from church.

"Eric, you know this lady?" Tristan said. Eric had a horrified look on his face . . . obviously things had gotten way out of hand.

"She . . . she's," Eric stuttered, "she's my sister, and that's her husband."

Through the commotion, security finally arrived.

"What do you mean that's her husband?" Tristan yelled. Anger surged through Tristan's body as he began to put the pieces of the puzzle together. "And you knew all along didn't you?" Tristan shouted. It all made sense now. "You were the one who was sending me those letters?" Tristan continued.

Suddenly, Tristan's mind went blank, and he lunged at Eric grabbing him around his neck ready for blood. Lisa who was crying over Brandon's body looked up and turned towards Eric and Tristan with fire in her eyes. No one noticed as she pulled a gun of her own from her purse. Security was trying to break up the fight between Eric and Tristan as everyone watched. There was a loud pop. The sound rang through the ears of everyone in close vicinity. Tristan's body went numb as he grabbed his back. He could feel a rush of cold blood run through him before he blacked out.

Lisa had fired a single bullet that entered Tristan's back. It lodged itself deep in his side. Seconds later, Lisa was tackled to the ground by security.

EPILOGUE

Tristan

I remembered . . . I remembered it all. The good times with my Sunday Brunch Club and the horrible times, like falling out with Rashawn and the effects his cancer had on everyone. I even remembered BJ. As I lay in the hospital bed in my mother's arms, I remembered it all. I remembered holding my new baby nephew and the bond I felt with him. I remembered the hope that little Alicia had given me and how much I loved her. I remembered laughing and playing with Corey and how much I enjoyed spending time with my brother. I remembered how much I loved my work and how blessed I was to get such an exciting job. I remembered all the feelings of despair and joy I had experienced in Atlanta. But I especially remembered the love I'd found in Michael. It's real. I know it because I could feel it in my body like warm water running through me.

I went in and out of consciousness as they rushed me to the hospital, and I remember Michael crying as I lay in the ICU. I could hear him saying over and over how he loved me and that he needed me to stay with him. I also remember my mother showing up what must have been hours later. Once she received the news, she was on the first flight out. She made it easy for me. I could feel her strength, and that made it easier for me to let go.

They say your life flashes before you when you die. Well, that's not true. Love flashed before me: Rashawn's laughter, Kim's beauty, my mother's strength, and the power of Michael's love.

You see just when I found the power of love . . . I died. But it's okay because I found what everyone looks for their whole life . . . I found love. And that love has carried me through to the other side.

I was in the ICU for a week, but the doctor's were hopeful for my recovery. They didn't, however, expect the massive internal bleeding that occurred as I lay in my mother's arms that day. It didn't hurt though, just a rush of coolness as I closed my eyes. I can still feel the wetness of my mother's tears as they landed on my head.

Just when . . . I thought to myself. Isn't that ironic?

ABOUT THE AUTHOR

A self proclaimed expert on contemporary African American literature, **G. L. Johnson** has studied a wide range of literature. Winning awards in creative writing, Johnson is happy to bring his first full length novel to the public. Born in Omaha, NE Johnson was raised on the North sided of Omaha, later moving to Atlanta, GA where he now resides. Here in Atlanta is where Johnson has been able to perfect his writing and began his career as an Author. Along with studying creative writing Johnson also studied education, and looked to be a teacher, however now works in property management.